THE CASE OF THE GIANT CARNIVOROUS WORM

A PENDLETON CASE: ONE

THOMAS E. STAPLES

Independent Publishing Network

United Kingdom

Thomas E. Staples
www.wrybrain.com

Publisher's Note: This is a work of fiction. Names, characters, places, and incidents are a product of the author's imagination. Locales and public names are sometimes used for atmospheric purposes. Any resemblance to actual people, living or dead, or to businesses, companies, events, institutions, or locales is completely coincidental.

The Case of the Giant Carnivorous Worm / Thomas E. Staples — 1st ed.

Print ISBN: 978-1-83853-114-0

eBook ISBN: 978-1-83853-115-7

GOING SOUTH

Naomi and Roberto were walking home late one evening as someone, or something, crept out from the storm-drain under the South Bridge. They didn't know what it was, but it didn't really matter because, in two minutes, Naomi's life would be over.

South Marshwood seemed to follow a trend of every significant bit of signposting appearing to have the word "South" shoved in front of it. South Bridge was technically down south, just below London, but there wasn't a North Bridge, or an East Bridge, or... you get the idea. Roberto always thought that it was originally built at the same time as a North Marshwood that never saw the light of day, thus explaining the name, whereas Naomi thought it was just because people in the past were really fucking stupid.

'I knew we should've brought a flashlight,' she said, kicking at the back of Roberto's heels as he walked over the bridge. 'I can't see sod all.'

'Nobody uses those anymore,' Roberto replied, chuckling to himself. 'Use your phone if it worries you.'

'I can't.'

'Why not?'

'The battery's almost out.'

'Brilliant,' said Roberto, pretending as if it wasn't his fault that her phone hadn't been charged properly, on account of him unplugging it to use his razor, and then forgetting to plug it back in afterwards. 'It's fine. It's not far.'

It was pretty far. The two of them weren't entirely sober as it was, making matters worse, as they'd come back from a bar their friend owned just shy of town and were understandably too pissed to drive.

Naomi didn't trust Roberto to drive in general, come to think of it.

'We should've got an Uber,' she went on, catching up to Roberto. 'Tightwad.'

'Don't be silly,' he replied. 'I can't afford that.'

He could.

'And I don't have the app.'

He did.

'And I'm not a tightwad!'

He really was.

'Okay,' she replied, puffing out her cheeks. 'Sure.'

Roberto grabbed her by the arm and pulled her closer towards him, just as the two came off the bridge and onto the most wood-like section of town. A lot of the trees were dead, what with it being December, but the tall, thick trunks still hid a lot of the town centre from sight.

The two stood still, wrapped in each other's arms, and Roberto kissed her on the lips. 'Are you okay?' he asked, smiling. He knew that, despite however mean they appeared to be to each other, that it wasn't genuine. 'Like, really okay?'

'I'm fine,' she replied, kissing him back. 'You always ask that.'

'Well, you know me. I'm always curious.'

Naomi puffed out her cheeks again. 'I'm just grumpy.'

'Right.'

'It is your fault, though.'

'Hey.' It didn't entirely seem like she was joking with that one. 'Arsehole.'

'Let's not stand around, then,' she said, shoving him forward and kicking him up the backside. 'Get a move on.'

The pair laughed, and after a moment, Roberto realised he was laughing on his own.

He turned around, his eyes still not completely adjusted to the dark and with little moonlight overhead to light the way, and frowned. 'Nay?' he asked, quietly. 'You alright?'

She didn't reply, and her shadowy figure was absent from where it should've been. That's when she screamed. It came from beneath the bridge and to the right where a steep incline led down onto the rocky ground below.

Roberto hesitated for a moment before tumbling down after her. Without the light to guide him, he slipped, his head smacking into a large rock and filling his eyes with stars. Blood leaked from his forehead as he found his footing, and he made his way towards Naomi's pleads for help as they echoed from the storm drain.

He heard a harsh, wet sound, like the tearing of flesh, and stumbled towards where it must've been coming from. He was too late, and as Roberto reached out to grab what he thought was Naomi, she was pulled screaming into the dark.

'Nay?' he asked, patting the ground in front of him until he felt something he could hold onto. 'You there?'

He picked the unknown object up and realised in the darkness that, with their wedding ring still attached to one of the fingers, it was Naomi's left hand.

CHAPTER ONE

PRIVATE DETECTIVE, PUBLIC NUISANCE

Anna was crouched in front of the opening to an empty outdoor dog kennel, picking at her chin with her fingers, when a woman in her mid-thirties came out to ask her what progress she'd made. As a surprise to no one, she'd made bugger all.

Standing up, Anna packed her long red hair into a bun behind her head and looked up to the sky. She wasn't looking for anything in particular, but the grey clouds that loomed overhead certainty weren't going to help matters. She was supposed to search for clues, look around a bit, and most importantly, find Joselyn's bloody Labrador.

These weren't going to be easy when it started pissing it down, and Anna knew this.

'Have you found anything yet, Miss Pendleton?' Joselyn asked, her voice as sweet as the cup of tea she was carrying. 'Here, I made you this. Eight sugars, just how you like it.'

'Ta,' said Anna, as she swiped the white cup off the tray and took a sip. 'And, nah, not yet. Workin' on it, though.'

Joselyn didn't doubt that, but she just wished that she'd been working on it a little faster. After all, Anna had been standing in Joselyn's garden for the last hour and had somehow managed to dart around erratically whilst pacing up and down, but without actually moving in any meaningful way.

It made Joselyn feel uneasy.

Crouching back down, Anna peered into the kennel again. 'So, you said you hadn't seen him since...?'

'Two nights ago,' Joselyn replied. 'The last time I saw him was when he came in for his dinner at six. He went outside and...'

'Never came back. Yes, I get it.' Anna rolled up the sleeve on her black raincoat and checked her watch. 'That was more than thirty hours ago. I wonder...' She started picking at her chin again, bolting upright and almost spilling the tea in her hand before downing the lot.

'You think you'll be able to find him, right?' Joselyn asked.

'Absolutely,' Anna replied, turning to face the woman much older than herself. 'Don't stress it, Jasmine.'

'It's Joselyn,' she added. 'Joselyn Chambers.'

Anna's eyes went wide as she slipped the mug back into Joselyn's hands. 'Oh yeah. I remember now.'

Don't fuck this up, she thought to herself. *You need this.*

'Your neighbours,' Anna asked, widely gesturing across the neighbourhood with her arms. 'What are they like?'

'They're fine,' Joselyn replied. 'I've never had any problems, but...'

'D'you think they might've stolen Bailey?'

'Bailey?'

'Your dog.'

'His name is Buddy, and no, that's ridiculous.'

Anna hummed to herself. 'Interesting. Leave it with me.'

'But for how long?' Joselyn asked. 'How long will you need?'

Anna blew a raspberry. 'I dunno, maybe until the end of the week? That should do it.'

'Isn't it Monday, though?' Joselyn rubbed her eyes together. 'That's quite a while and...'

'Listen, do you want me to find Bobby or not?' said Anna. 'You'll get your monies worth, I promise.'

Joselyn sighed. 'Well, okay, but you'll at least keep me updated, won't you?'

'Of course I will,' said Anna, her smile a little too overbearing. 'I'll get right to work.'

Joselyn's face was much lower going into the house than it had been when she'd come out of it, but once she was out of sight, Anna did as she promised and got to work.

Once she'd finished biting her lip, Anna raised her right hand towards the sky and dragged the sun to the west until it was out of sight, plunging the back garden into darkness. Looking down at her watch with furrowed brows, the time skipped from two in the afternoon to six in the afternoon, and the date went back two days. With the sky almost entirely black, Anna snapped her fingers and the lights in Joselyn's back garden switched on, lighting up both herself and the dog kennel.

None of this was actually happening, of course. It was still two in the afternoon, the sun was still up and Buddy was still missing, but that information wasn't useful to Anna. She needed to set the scene, after all, which she continued to do inside her own head. To Joselyn, Anna was just flailing her arms about in her garden and snapping her fingers, looking rather mental, indeed.

Anna turned towards the house — the moon hidden in the night sky — and watched as Buddy strolled out of it towards the top of the garden, cocked his leg up a tree, and then set-tled down in his kennel. She looked up at the surrounding houses.

'People would've been up,' she whispered to herself. 'Sure-ly.'

She clapped her hands together and the neighbouring windows burst into a faint yellow light, some with silhou-ettes, and some without. Anna looked down at the dog, and in return, the dog lifted its head off the ground, tilting it to the side.

'Now, where did you go?' Anna asked herself.

Joselyn's garden was much wider than it was long, and the dog's kennel, while not exactly large either, was pushed against the wooden fence towards the back as to not take up any extra room.

Anna scoured the fence. It was well-maintained and hole free, so, Buddy couldn't have gotten out that way. Crouching down beside it, Anna ran her hands across the ground be-neath the fence, also finding no gaps under there. Buddy couldn't have gotten out that way, either, and the fence didn't look particularly climbable, especially for a dog of that size.

Anna returned to the kennel and, after waving her hands about, the sun re-appeared in the sky and her watch reset to its original, correct time. She closed her eyes for a moment, and once she'd re-opened them, Buddy was gone and the kennel was empty.

She crawled inside, and Joselyn watched from the kitchen window, vaguely concerned for the young girls' sanity.

Using the knuckle of her index finger, Anna tapped all around the inside of the kennel, on the ceiling, the wall, and at last, the floor. Every tap made a quick, sharp noise that ended as quickly as it began until she struck a section of the floorboard that rang out differently from all the other parts.

She tapped it again. The sound was distant; hollow.

'Bingo,' she said, and once she crawled back out of the kennel, she heaved it across the garden, leaving a rectangle of flattened grass where it used to be.

Joselyn didn't like that, and she came charging back into the garden. 'What have you done?' she asked.

That snapped Anna out of it. 'There's something under it,' she said. 'Or, not under it, even.'

Within the centre of the rectangle left behind by the kennel was a hole about one metre across and countless more deep.

'Wait...' said Joselyn, walking over to it. 'I—'

'That ain't because of you, is it?' she asked, pointing into the hole. 'Figured. You've got a sinkhole.'

'How did that get there?'

'I dunno. How do they get anywhere?' she quickly replied, tugging at her own neck and pinching the skin. 'One problem at a time.' She turned to Joselyn and snapped her fingers at her. 'Get me some water.'

'What? Why?'

'Don't argue. Just do it,' Anna replied. 'Lots of water. A bucket'll do.'

'Okay.'

'Better yet, you got a hosepipe?'

Joselyn nodded.

'Fetch that.'

The older woman left to do as Anna had told her, even if she wasn't particularly happy about it.

She returned with the hose.

'Okay,' said Anna, slapping her legs to a tune that Joselyn didn't recognise. 'Shove it in the hole.'

'What?' Joselyn replied. 'Why?'

'What did I say earlier?'

'Don't argue...?'

'Exactly. Go on, then.'

'Okay,' said Joselyn, at last, regretting her decision to hire this nutcase. 'If you think it's a good idea.'

'Trust me. It is.'

She fed the yellow line down into the hole until it hit the bottom, before storming over to the tap and switching it on, filling it with water.

'Now we wait,' said Anna, getting her phone out almost instantly and searching through her Twitter directs.

They were empty.

She slipped her phone back into her pocket and peered into the hole, watching as the muddy water slowly rose to the surface, carrying something with it.

Anna looked closer. 'There's something in 'ere,' she said, getting on her knees and reaching down into the pit. 'Gotcha!'

She pulled her hand out and in her grasp was a muddy, damp dog collar with blood dried into the fabric.

Joselyn's face drained itself of fluid. 'Is that...'

'Yep,' Anna replied, not seeming to care anywhere near as much. 'Here you go.'

She tossed it over to Joselyn, who fumbled it for a moment before catching it, and hoisted the hose out of the pit. 'Right, my work here is done,' she said, with a smile. 'Make sure you forward the cash to my PayPal, yeah?'

'But, how did he get under the kennel? Nobody moved it.'

'No idea, mate,' said Anna, brushing it off. 'At least you know what happened to him. These bloody sinkholes, honestly, must've suffocated the poor bastard. Anyway, my advice is to...'

'I don't want your fucking advice!' Joselyn barked. 'I want you to leave. Now.'

'You what?' Anna replied. 'I found your...'

'Get out!'

'Alright.' Anna's eyes widened. 'Let's just calm down.'

'I'm calling the police.'

Anna left pretty quickly after that, still peering into Joselyn's front door. 'I'm still getting paid, right?' she asked, trying that smile again as the sky opened and the rain fell.

Joselyn slammed the door in her face and locked it.

'Tell your friends!' Anna shouted. 'Dammit.'

I don't get it. Did I upset her?

That thought was a fleeting one as Anna scrolled through her phone to open up her bank details, finding that she was still about a half a grand shy of where she needed to be, and had to go home empty-handed, once again, and face the wrath of her landlord.

She just needed the right case. That was all. One she could solve without sending the client into orbit or giving them a panic attack. One that would pay the bills for, well, a month or two, at least. One that would cause everyone in South Marshwood to know her name, and not associate it with the crazy ginger girl that acts as if she's being constantly electrocuted.

That case was coming, and if Anna had known that ahead of time, she'd have probably chosen a safer career path.

CHAPTER TWO

THE PEEPING TOM

Jon Peterson was staring at Angela at half past nine in the evening, from a hedge, just outside her kitchen window. Angela was unaware, of course, tending to her usual business of making a cup of tea and forgetting to feed the cat.

With the lights on, Angela couldn't see a thing that was happening in the outside world, whereas the outside world — including Jon, who hadn't moved from his cold, prickly hedge since half past seven — could see everything that she was up to. Creeping on Angela had since become a hobby of Jon's, although he wouldn't admit to in public, for obvious reasons. Her house was about a mile from his own, several streets over, and as he had no desire to shit where he ate, he was more than okay with that.

What Angela would've thought of it didn't matter to him, if she even knew his name to begin with. He didn't see a problem with what he was doing; to him, nobody was being harmed.

Angela flicked the switch on the bottom of the white kettle and it roared into life, with Jon even hearing it from within the confines of his favourite hedge as he looked on. She ducked down out of sight, re-appearing a moment later with a glass mug and teabag.

Two sugars, Jon thought to himself, his breath visible in the cold. *Cubed.*

Angela took out a packet of sugar cubes and tossed two of them into the mug. Jon smiled, until she decided to add a third one, and then he didn't. She turned away from the window and walked back into the darkness of the living room, away from Jon's gaze. Sitting down on the sofa as the kettle rumbled behind her, Angela fumbled around for the remote to the TV.

It wasn't where she left it, nor did she know where the hell that actually was in the first place, so she got up and went looking. The light switch wasn't worth fumbling around for as the lightbulb it'd been connected to had died three weeks ago, so Angela waited for her eyes to adjust before waving her hands around the room, feeling for every surface that made sense to her at the time.

Jon, still outside, was getting impatient. He knew he didn't have much time left to spy on Angela, on account of her moving in a week's time after a sinkhole appeared in her bathroom and swallowed her toilet, so he crawled out of the hedge and towards the window, peering in with his hands pressed against the glass.

That's when he saw it.

Angela had found the remote and thrown herself back onto the sofa as the kettle was nearing its boil. She flicked the TV on, the bright light revealing three silhouettes to Jon who, having studied her home with frightening detail, realised that couldn't be right.

There was Angela and her cat; two living things, two silhouettes.

So, why were there three?

Angela stood up. The kettle was boiled, and as she walked back into the kitchen, Jon took a step backwards as to not give himself away. She poured the water into the mug and stirred the bag around, adding a splash of milk in afterwards. She tossed the bag in the bin and turned back to the living room where the extra figure was waiting for her.

Jon panicked. What could he do? He could call the police, sure, but how would he explain what he'd seen? He couldn't let onto what he'd been getting up to once the sun went down. His life would be ruined.

It was probably nothing. Angela was fine. Jon was fine. Everything was fine.

On the TV, some violent, straight to *Netflix* gangster movie was playing, and it'd just gotten to a moment where the two mobs in town had come together to discuss business, and almost definitely shoot the ever-living shit out of each other.

The latter came quickly, and Angela's living room lit up in the flashes of the gunfire. Jon could see her sitting in her chair, with the cat standing beside her and bumping its head into her shins.

Flash.

The cat was gone, as if they'd disappeared between frames in a horror movie.

Flash.

The silhouette, the unknown one, was beside Angela's chair. Its shape was... wrong. Jon didn't have a clue what it was, and a moment later...

Flash.

...it had disappeared, along with Angela's head and the inside of her stomach.

Her body was splayed across the carpet, decapitated, with liquid oozing out of every hole in her body and — as the TV burst into a bright light once again — Jon realised that there were plenty of those.

He screamed. He stumbled backwards. He fell into his favourite hedge.

The thin branches crumpled under his weight as some seemed to claw at his arms, before he crawled his way out and into the open. He stood up, sweating, and took out his phone. He'd never dialled the emergency services before and even hesitated before doing so, until he considered that this was most definitely an emergency.

He told them about the intruder, the address of the house, and to come as quick as possible. He left out the bit about him hiding in a bush, though, obviously. He didn't need that, but what he did need was to get the fuck out of there.

He knew the quickest way back to his house was through the garden and over the neighbouring fences, so that's where he went. The fences weren't tall, and the square pattern in the woodwork helped him hoist himself up and over them.

Jon ran, clearing the first fence before he heard a crash come from behind him. He turned around; a mistake, as it slowed him down. The back door to Angela's house, which led into the extension she'd had built a couple of years ago, now had a giant hole where the cat flap should've been.

'Fuck,' Jon said to himself. 'That must be one big cat.'

He turned on his heels and kept running, digging his fingers into the fence across from him and hauling himself over it, snagging three splinters along the way. Whatever was behind him, though, didn't care much for others personal property, and was just charging straight through the wooden panels.

Jon emerged on the street opposite and stumbled onto the dimly lit pathway, the pattering of feet following close behind him. Tripping over the curb and landing flat on his face under a streetlamp, Jon rolled himself over, sweating buckets as he scampered to his feet and saw the shadow leap towards him. Jon only felt two things after that; something hitting him, and then him hitting the ground.

Once his eyes were open again, it was already the morning. The night had passed him by without him even realising it. He was alive, which was lucky, but covered in a thick layer of green, smelly goo.

He stood up, confused, afraid, and carried on running.

CHAPTER THREE

YOUR RENT IS DUE

Anna Pendleton's apartment was complete and utter shit.

By moving away from her family almost as soon as she was old enough to do so, it's no surprise that Anna was as horrifically unprepared for life alone as she was, and for the last three years, she'd been paying for it in spades.

Or, rather, not paying for it.

The scuff marks on her navy blue carpet had been a point of concern, for one, as they certainly weren't like that when she moved in at eighteen years old. She was twenty-one, now, and it'd only gotten worse since her constant rushing about rarely gave her time to even take her shoes off; a price that the carpet had evidently paid over time.

The first room, one of three, narrowly stretched back a dozen or so meters with a door off to the left side, leading to the rest of the apartment. Aside from that, there was little else to it. The kitchen had been merged with the front room, and everything useful such as the washing machine or the oven had been stuck under the worktop to make more use of the space.

Beyond that, Anna's apartment only had one window. It was above the teabag stained sink, and lying ahead of it was a view of some low trees and a single road; a view that most people would describe as "just okay."

Anna was stood in the middle of her living room, if you could call it that, with her laptop balanced on one arm as she scrolled through her Twitter with the other. It wasn't just her Twitter, mind you, she had about four separate tabs all clogging the screen at once, including her email, which was empty, her LinkedIn, which had the same problem, and the official Pendleton sub-reddit; having still gained zero traction since she set it up a few days prior.

There was a knock at the door, and Anna slid her laptop onto the one spare bit of worktop before almost dropping it entirely.

I have a doorbell, she thought. *Why does nobody use the doorbell?*

There was another knock. She answered it.

'Hey, Steve!' said Anna, arms outstretched. 'How's it going?'

The man sighed. 'It's Stanley, not Steve,' he said, disappointed. 'I'm here for the rent money. You said you'd have it, remember?'

Anna's face dropped. 'Ah, yes, I do remember saying that.'

'Do you have it?'

'Well,' said Anna, her eyes darting to the top right of her head. 'It's a long story.'

'Okay, go on.'

'I don't have it.'

'And?'

'That's it.'

'That's the story?'

'Yes.'

Stanley brought his fingers up to his eyeballs and pinched them together. 'You know I'm going to have to kick you out, right?'

'What?' said Anna. 'Come on, this is only the second time I've missed a payment.'

'I'm allowed to evict after the first,' he replied. 'And this is your third, actually.'

'No,' said Anna, with certainty. 'Really?'

Stanley produced a folder from the messenger bag slung over his shoulder and pulled out a folder. 'Let's take a look, shall we?'

Anna's face went red. 'Okay,' she said, picking at her chin. 'Sure, let's take a look. Would you like to come in? Cup of tea, maybe? I'd offer you a seat, but—'

'I'm fine out here,' said Stanley, not taking his eyes off the document in his hands. 'Ah, here we go.'

Shit.

'In March you were eight days late for a payment of five hundred and fifty pounds and thirty-six pence, and then, in July, you were twelve days late for the same.'

'Well, yeah, whatever,' said Anna. 'But, you got your money, didn't you?'

'That's not the point,' said Stanley, narrowing his eyes. 'And don't "yeah, whatever" me.'

'Yeah, yeah, whatever,' Anna replied. 'What's your point?'

'The point is that I'm your landlord, you're staying in my building, and you owe me the rent money that I am due *on time.*'

'Well, how much do I owe you, then?'

Stanley pulled out another document and flicked it on top of the first. 'Seven hundred and eighty-four pounds.'

'What the fuck?' Anna asked, stumbling backwards into her living room. 'Why?'

'And thirty-two pence,' he went on. 'The price went up two months ago, Anna. You were aware of this.'

'Bollocks was I.'

Stanley handed the paper over to Anna that – once she took hold of it – explained in considerable detail that the monthly rent was going up.

'I didn't sign this!' she said.

Stanley tapped at the bottom of the page with a pen, showing a signature that looked like a spider had been dipped in ink and thrown at the paper, which meant that, yes, Anna had indeed signed it.

'Piss,' said Anna, as her chest sank and she handed the contract back. 'Listen, I can get you the money.'

'You said this last time,' Stanley replied. 'And the time before that.'

'And I got the money, didn't I? I know, it's bad, but I was supposed to be getting paid today and I got dicked over.'

'So?'

'So,' she said, itching her face. 'They're gonna pay me next week, and then you'll get your money.'

'Anna...'

'C'mon, dude,' she said. 'This'll be the last time. Please?'

Stanley's eyes shot to the ceiling as he sighed into his folder, slipping it back into his bag afterwards. 'This is the last time,' he went on. 'You have seven days, and if you aren't going to have my money by then, well, you might as well spend that time looking for somewhere else to live.'

'Got it,' said Anna, giving the thumbs up with both hands. 'Seven days.'

'Seven-hundred and eighty-four pounds...'

'Seven-hundred and eighty-four pounds.'

'And thirty-two pence...'

'And thirty-two pence. Consider it done.'

'I'll consider it done when I see it,' said Stanley. 'Don't let me down.'

He turned away from Anna and walked down the brown, energy-less hallway as a tall, short-haired brunette with a chequered flannel passed him on his way to the elevator.

'Hello, Stanley,' she said, with a smile.

Stanley just kept walking.

Anna peered out from her open door towards the woman and signalled her inside with a flappy hand gesture. 'Get in, Maddie,' she whispered. 'I'm in trouble.'

'Nothing new there,' Maddie replied. 'What's up?'

Anna grabbed ahold of Maddie and pulled her into her apartment, slamming the door behind her.

'I like your new sign,' said Maddie. 'Very professional.'

'Yeah, whatever,' Anna quickly blurted, running her hands up and down her face.

'What's wrong?' Maddie asked. 'Something happen?'

'I'm knackered,' she said. 'I've got a first-class ticket on the Fucked Express to Buggery Town.'

There was a pause.

'I don't know what any of that means,' said Maddie. 'You need to chill out. What's the problem?'

Maddie was always chilled out in comparison to Anna, but then again, anyone would look chilled out in comparison to Anna.

'Bloody Steve just came over asking for the rent, didn't he?' said Anna, pacing around the room. 'What am I gonna do?'

'Steve?' Maddie asked. 'You mean Stanley?'

'Yeah, whatever. Stanley. He came asking for his money.'

'Well, that's fair enough,' said Maddie. 'He is actually your landlord.'

Anna blew a raspberry. 'I haven't got the money.'

'Not surprisingly,' said Maddie, making herself at home on the floor. 'You don't have a job.'

'I have a job!'

'But, like, a real job, though.'

'A private investigator is a real job,' said Anna. 'Thank you very much.'

'Alright, sorry,' Maddie added, crossing her legs. 'How did things go with your client?'

'Not well. Not well at all.'

'Did you solve it?'

'Yeah, I solved it,' said Anna. 'But she just got all pissy about it when she found out her dog was dead.'

Maddie sat in silence, and Anna noticed.

'What are you doing?' Anna asked.

'What?'

'That face,' she said. 'You're judging me. I feel a judgement. That's your judging face.'

'Well,' said Maddie, 'you're not exactly the best when it comes to dealing with stuff like that, are you?'

'What are you on about?'

'You're not what I'd call the most sensitive soul...'

'So,' said Anna. 'Why should that matter?'

'Because she lost a pet she probably cared a great deal about. Did you, y'know, comfort her at all?'

'That's not my job.'

'Perhaps it should be.'

'Whatever,' said Anna, stomping around the room. 'Anyway, why are you here?'

'I thought I'd stop by to see if you were coming out tonight.'

'Where?' Anna asked, quickly. 'And with who?'

'Just out.'

'With who?' she asked again. 'People?'

'Yes,' said Maddie. 'People.'

'Nah, I'm good. Besides, I can't afford it.'

Maddie raised an eyebrow. 'We won't go out, then,' she said. 'You can just come over, spend the night with me. We'll order a pizza.'

'I can't afford it.'

'*I'll* order the pizza,' she corrected herself. 'Come on, it'll be fun.'

'What kind of fun?'

Maddie didn't answer that. She knew what kind she was secretly hoping for, but just having Anna there would be enough for her.

'Anyway, I can't. I need to figure this shit out, first. Otherwise, I'm gonna be homeless by the end of the week.'

'You're not going to be homeless.'

'I'm gonna be living in a dumpster.'

'You're not going to be living in a dumpster.' Maddie looked around. 'Although, it looks like you already are. I mean, who doesn't have a sofa? And you should really turn this light on.' She reached up to flick the light switch. Nothing happened. 'Jesus, Anna.'

'All that stuff slows me down,' said Anna. 'Don't want it. Don't need it.'

'You're mad.'

'Sure. Coffee?'

'I'll make it,' said Maddie, standing herself up. 'You always spill it with your constant jitters.'

Maddie stepped foot onto the wooden section of flooring that encompassed the kitchen area of Anna's apartment, and noticed how much of it was covered in stains from when coffee had been splattered across the floor.

'I don't have jitters,' said Anna, snapping her fingers for no reason whatsoever. 'I'm just energetic.'

'You're a spaz, is what you are,' said Maddie, reaching the worktop and looking puzzled.

'Furthest cupboard on the left.'

There were three to choose from. Maddie opened the leftmost one and found the tube of instant coffee granules. 'Cheers,' she said, pulling out two mugs and spooning the granules into them. 'One sugar or two?'

'Eight,' said Anna. 'Ta.'

'What on earth?'

'What?'

'Eight sugars?'

'Yeah?' Anna shrugged. 'What's the problem?'

'Don't worry,' replied Maddie, after a slight pause. 'It doesn't matter.' She peered over at Anna's laptop as she tossed a handful of sugar cubes into a pale mug. 'Any new clients?'

'Dunno, yet,' said Anna, fumbling her phone out of her pocket. 'No emails, no tweets, no calls; nothing. I'm screwed.'

'Well, my offer is still open,' Maddie replied. 'Only if you're desperate, obviously.'

'It's fine. I'm not gonna need to move in with you.'

'It'd be cheaper,' said Maddie, hiding her disappointment. 'Less hassle.'

'I like my privacy. Thanks, though.'

'Anytime.' The kettle had finished boiling, and Maddie started pouring the water into the mugs when a knock came at the door, making her jump. 'Who's that? Jesus.'

'Nah, I don't think it's him,' Anna replied, marching over to the door. 'Stewart's probably back again.'

'Stewart?' Maddie asked. 'Who's that?'

'Sorry, I meant Steve. My landlord.'

'You mean Stanley.'

'That's the one,' said Anna, snapping her fingers and pointing at Maddie. 'Parasitic bastard.'

'I like Stanley. He's a nice man.'

'He's a tosspot.'

'Well, he's still giving you some leeway. Give the guy a break. Answer the door, too.'

'I was going to,' said Anna, flapping her arms about. 'Look, this is me, answering the door.' She placed her hand on the doorknob and twisted it. 'I already told you,' she began, 'I'll have your rent by the end of the...'

It wasn't Stanley. It was some guy that neither Anna nor Maddie had seen before, and once he collapsed onto the carpet of Anna's apartment, they weren't even sure if he was still alive or not.

'I didn't say you could come in,' said Anna, failing to catch him. 'Rude.'

'Oh, Jesus,' Maddie replied, dropping what she was doing and rushing over to the man. 'Are you okay?'

'He's probably fine.'

'He's bleeding, and he's—' A thick strand of slime came off in her hands. 'He's covered in this weird green stuff.'

'Oh, gross.'

'You might have a new client,' said Maddie, checking his pulse before she reached into the pocket of the man's jeans and pulled out his wallet. Looking inside, she found his license.

'Who is he?' Anna asked. 'What's the guy's name?'

Maddie turned the license towards Anna. 'Jon Peterson,' she said. 'Do you know him?'

CHAPTER FOUR

EVERYTHING SOUNDS BETTER IN THE BOG

A couple of builders had arrived at Angela's house the morning after she'd been murdered to find that the place had been covered in yellow tape, best suited to a crime scene. They didn't pay much attention to it, of course, as they had a job to do, and figured whatever must've happened wouldn't cause them any problems.

They weren't very smart.

Gabriel, the bigger builder, crept under the yellow tape and through the front door, hauling a sledgehammer behind his head. Derek, who was much scrawnier and with a considerably larger beard, followed close behind with a toolbox in either hand. They'd both been scheduled to figure out what on earth was going on with the sinkhole that'd appeared in Angela's bathroom, so, they brought every tool imaginable in the hopes that they could sort it out.

Finding the bathroom, Derek and Gabriel wandered inside and slammed their tools down on the tiled floor, cracking it further than it already had been by the giant hole in the centre of the room. The hole was bigger than they'd been lead to believe, spanning a couple of metres across and descending down far enough that they couldn't see the bottom of it.

'Let's plug this bastard up,' said Gabriel, 'and let's get the hell out of here.'

Derek nodded and stepped out of the bathroom, returning a moment later with a large bucket of quick-set liquid cement. He got to work, mixing it up until the bucket almost weighed a tonne and they could start filling the sinkhole.

'I wonder how deep it goes,' said Derek, peering into the darkness.

'I don't really give a shit,' Gabriel replied, sternly. 'Like, at all.'

Gabriel and Derek weren't very good friends, but they tolerated each other as, well, they didn't have many other options.

'Fill it up.'

He did, hoisting the bucket over the edge of the hole. The thick grey cement began to ooze from the ridges of the plastic and down into the sinkhole, splattering across the bottom of which they were unable to see.

That's when a noise came from beneath them. It was faint, and were it not for the vibrations that Derek felt under his feet, they might have not noticed it at all.

'Do you hear that?' Derek asked.

'Huh?' Gabriel replied, eating a cheese sandwich. 'Hear what?'

Derek focused his ears and stopped pouring the cement. 'Sounds like a rat,' he said, eventually. 'A rat scuttling under the floorboards.'

'What floorboards, mate?' Gabriel added. 'This is all dirt and stone.'

'Then it's a rat borrowing through the dirt,' said Derek. 'But, louder.'

'Just don't worry about it. We're not here to worry. Keep pouring that shit.'

He did as Gabriel told him, and tipped all of the cement out of the bucket until the hole was half-filled. 'Shit.'

Gabriel sighed. 'Go and fetch the other one, then,' he said. 'Chop-chop, I wanna get outta here.'

So he did. Ducking under all the yellow crime scene tape and out towards the van, Derek spotted a car parked up in the driveway. It was a white *Vauxhall Astra*; a police car. That wasn't strange, exactly. The strange part came when Derek couldn't find whoever had been driving it.

Derek was worried that something was wrong, but as Gabriel had not-so-kindly pointed out earlier, it wasn't his job to worry, so he hauled the second bucket of cement out of the back of their van and painfully dragged it into the bathroom.

'About time,' said Gabriel, who was still leaning on his sledgehammer, having not moved an inch. 'Hurry up.'

A short time later, Derek had filled the sinkhole to the surface, before flattening out the cement with a trowel.

'Good as new,' said Gabriel. 'Looks great.'

It looked like shit.

'Let's get outta here.'

'Wait,' said Derek, bringing his ear close to the ground. 'I can hear something again. It's right underneath us.'

'Mate, nobody cares,' said Gabriel. 'Our job is done. Let's bail.'

Derek sighed. 'Alright, if you say so.'

'If we're lucky, might have time to grab something from *Greggs* on the way,' Gabriel added, turning towards the bathroom door. 'Come on.'

'But, you've just eaten.'

'I can eat again. Let's get outta here.'

He had almost made it out of the bathroom when the ground opened up beneath his feet, swallowing his lower half before he even realised it. The sledgehammer went flying away from him, skidding across the ground. Gabriel and Derek both screamed over each other one as panic set in.

'FUCK!' Gabriel yelled. 'Help me, then!'

'I'm fucking trying!' Derek yelled back. 'Gimme both your arms.'

Gabriel started spitting blood as both his hands were interlocked with Derek's. He used all his strength to yank his colleague out of the sinkhole, which he found to be a bit easier than he was expecting, considering Gabriel's size when compared to his.

That, as Derek soon found out, was because he'd only lifted Gabriel's upper half out of the sinkhole. A large streak of red was left behind Gabriel as his intestines flapped about beneath his waist; right where his legs should've been.

'Oh, shit,' said Derek. 'Oh, shit. Oh, shit. Oh, shit.'

'What is it?' Gabriel spluttered, refusing to look around. 'Am I okay?' His eyes leaked blood, and a moment later, his breathing stopped.

Derek let him go, and as he looked into the sinkhole that'd just appeared beneath them, a spindly black appendage crept out from the darkness, skewering a hole in Gabriel's back and dragging the rest of his body into it, leaving nothing more than a smear of blood across the pale bathroom tiles. Derek scurried backwards on all fours, trying to create a distance between himself and the sinkhole. He reached for the sledgehammer – thinking it'd do some good – grabbing it just in time to force himself off of the ground and out of the bathroom.

Gripping his weapon tightly, Derek heard something scuttling behind him as whatever it was drew closer. He didn't

turn around. Running forward, Derek dashed up the staircase and into one of the bedrooms.

You moron, he thought. *You trapped yourself.*

He wasn't wrong. There was no way out, so, instead, he
looked for a place to hide. He could've slid under the bed, but
whatever was behind him was likely to check that place first,
so the cupboard would have to do.

His hands slipped off the handle from all the sweat on his
palms, until he tried again, yanking the cupboard door open
and slinking his way inside, closing it behind him with his
sledgehammer held closely to his chest. There was a slight
crack between the two thin, wooden doors he was hidden behind, and through it, he saw something enter the bedroom.

At first he heard a squeak and assumed it was just the
door in need of some serious WD40, but when the squeak
continued, higher and higher in pitch as it crept closer to the
cupboard he was hiding in, he knew it wasn't that.

What the fuck is that thing? he thought, holding his
breath. *What the fuck is that?*

He'd never seen anything like it. The creature left a streak
of blood wherever it wandered as strips of flesh hung from its
mandibles. The wooden floor beneath it made the pitter-
patter of pointed limbs all the more chilling, sending a sharp
bolt down Derek's spine.

He rested his head against the business end of the sledgehammer.

He could take it, right? It was just a pest; a vermin. Granted, it was about the size of a Great Dane, with considerably
more eyes, but nothing a sledgehammer couldn't fix.

As he met the creature's gaze with his own, the room went
silent. He'd seen it, and as all six of the thing's legs bent and
twitched in tandem, he was almost certain it'd seen him, too.

He gripped the sledgehammer tightly, tried to force his heart back down into his chest, and waited to die.

CHAPTER FIVE

HOSPITALITY

One of the boils on Jon Peterson's skin burst open and spilt green liquid across the hospital bed he'd been laid down on. Covering his body, the pus-like gunk seemed to bubble beneath his skin in lumps of different shapes and sizes.

It was gross.

Anna and Maddie watched as a team of doctors and nurses wheeled Jon away up the corridor and into an emergency room. Maddie pulled Anna aside. 'What are you thinking?' she asked. 'Any theories?'

Anna was running her fingers down her chin, as if she were deep in thought, before she spoke. 'Aliens.'

'What?' Maddie replied, stumbling backwards. 'You can't be serious.'

'It's possible,' said Anna, her face failing to indicate whether she was actually joking or not. 'I wouldn't be surprised.'

Why are you like this? Maddie thought but didn't say. *I need more friends my age.*

'What is happening?' she asked. 'How does that guy know you? How do you even know anyone?'

'I don't,' Anna replied. 'I've never seen him before in my life.'

'But he knew where you lived.'

Anna shrugged. 'So?'

'Please don't tell me you advertise your address online.'

'Okay,' said Anna, picking at her chin. 'It's entirely possible that I do.'

'Jesus Christ,' said Maddie, sighing into her hands. 'You're an idiot.'

'What's the worst that can happen?'

'A half-dead man arrived at your door less than an hour ago. I'd say that's pretty bad.'

Anna blew a raspberry. 'We got him the help he needed,' she said, reaching into her pocket and pulling out a small, scrunched up piece of paper. 'And I got this.'

'What is that?' Maddie whispered. 'Did you steal it?'

'Yes,' Anna replied. 'Pinched it from his wallet. Thought it might come in handy.'

Maddie frowned and led Anna into an empty area of the hospital corridor. 'You can't just steal the poor guy's wallet,' she whispered. 'What is wrong with you?'

'He's not gonna need it, is he?' she replied. 'He's dead.'

'Half-dead.'

'Same difference. Besides, I didn't steal his wallet. I picked up the wallet, stole the thing from inside of said wallet, and then gave the wallet back. What's the problem?'

Maddie sighed. 'What does it say?'

'It's an address; must be his. I'm gonna go and check it out.'

Anna spun on her heels and went to leave the hospital when Maddie grabbed her by the elbow and pulled her back in. 'I'm coming, too,' she said. 'I want to see what this is about.'

'Absolutely not,' Anna replied, pushing her away. 'It could be dangerous.'

'Exactly. Let's go.'

'You're not coming, end of. You'll distract me. Besides, I need you for something else.'

'Oh yeah?' Maddie asked. 'And what's that?'

***

Back in her apartment, Anna dumped her laptop in-front of Maddie's face as if it were weightless, and pointed her towards all of the open, empty tabs littering her screen.

'I'm not being your receptionist,' said Maddie, picking the laptop up and sliding it across the floor. 'That's degrading.'

'I wasn't thinking a receptionist, so much,' Anna replied, pacing around the room. 'I was thinking more of a sexy secretary.'

Maddie went red. 'What do you want me to do?'

'Just keep track of everything that's going on,' said Anna, miming a mini-keyboard in her hands, 'and text me when you hear something.'

'What counts as something?' Maddie asked.

'I dunno. You'll know it when you see it.'

Maddie slammed the lid of the laptop closed and stood up off the floor. 'I really think it'd be best if I came with you to this place. If something goes wrong I want to be there with you.'

'Nah, it's fine,' Anna replied, waving her hand as if to brush the suggestion away, before hammering the newfound address into Google Maps. 'I work better alone.'

'So you keep saying.'

The location of the address Anna entered into her phone appeared on screen, showing it to only be a fifteen-minute

walk from her apartment at most. Anna tossed her phone onto the worktop, unlocked, and bounded over towards the
bathroom for a wee. Whilst she was gone, Maddie reached
for the phone and, too, saw where the address would lead
Anna. She took a screenshot of it, texted it to herself, and
then set the phone back where it was before Anna came back
into the living room; just as a precaution.

'Right,' said Anna, slipping her phone into her pocket. 'I'm
off. Keep me posted, yeah?'

'Yeah,' Maddie replied. 'Whatever.'

Anna didn't like that line being used on herself, so she just
chose to ignore it. There was a job to do.

'You're probably not going to get paid for this, y'know,'
said Maddie. 'On account of the guy being in a coma.'

Anna pulled the front door open. 'I know,' she said, stepping out into the hallway. 'That's why I pinched his debit
card.' The door slammed shut.

'Unbelievable,' Maddie said to herself. 'Unbelievable.'

CHAPTER SIX

GABRIEL'S SLEDGEHAMMER

Anna arrived at what she thought was Jon Peterson's house, failing to realise that it actually belonged to a woman named Angela, who'd been torn to pieces the night before. The yellow tape that both Gabriel and Derek had seen before at least one of them suffered the same fate was still there, too, and now there were two vehicles outside instead of one: the police car and the creepy builders van.

If Anna had known what she was getting herself into, she wouldn't have wandered into the nest of something she didn't understand, but she didn't, and so she did.

Stepping through into the living room, Anna saw a weak, orange coloured patch on the carpet beside the settee. It was quite faint, and the carpet itself was already a light brown, so most people would've missed it at a first glance, but of course, Anna wasn't most people. She hopped down onto her knees and crawled over to the stain, running her hands up and down the carpet to feel the roughness of it.

Conclusion; it was most definitely a carpet.

The section where the orange stain sat felt sticky to the touch, with the singular fibres of it being glued together. Anna sniffed it. It smelled like metal, and after she licked it, she found that it tasted like it, too. She stood up, took a step back, and focused her mind, rebuilding the scene in her head.

Looking down at her watch she saw that it was nearing five in the afternoon, and with the quick wave of her hand, it now informed her that it was about half past ten at night. She snapped her fingers and the light in the room disappeared, and when she snapped them again the TV came on.

Who Wants to be a Millionaire? was showing.

That's not right, she thought to herself, waving her hand back and forth in front of the television until the channel changed to something more suitable, landing on *Jurassic Park,* her favourite movie. She smiled. *That'll do.*

The next thing that she needed to figure out was where the stain had come from. Being almost certain it was blood, Anna needed a body, and so she imagined Maddie lying face down as red liquid gushed from a hole in her skull. This wasn't accurate to the real events, and Anna knew that, but that part wasn't important. If she were to visualise this properly, she needed a body, and hers had to do.

Now, she thought, *how did that body get there?*

The blood spraying from the hole in Maddie's head was suddenly sucked back into her skull before the wound itself was sealed shut. She stood up, walked back towards the settee, and slumped down into it.

Then Anna pulled out a gun and shot her in the head. The blood sprayed out of the side of Maddie's skull as her skin flapped about, covering the settee and dribbling red onto the floor.

Time froze.

'No,' Anna said to herself. 'It's not quite right. The splatter patterns are way off.'

Time went backwards. The chunks of brain were sucked back into Maddie's head before she carried on watching the same scene of *Jurassic Park* she'd watched five seconds ago. It was the part where the chubby guy gets his face torn off by the Dilophosaurus, which just so happened to be Anna's favourite bit.

Anna put the handgun back into her coat pocket, before pulling out a shotgun like one of Tommy Cooper's magic tricks. She pressed it against Maddie's head and, as same as before, pulled the trigger. The side of her head came off and the exit wound looked like a floppy lasagne, but it still wasn't quite right. There wasn't just blood on the settee, as Anna noted, but there was also a pool of blood around it, too, so she would've fallen towards her, rather than away.

Time rewound again, as Anna put her final idea into action.

She pressed a knife she didn't have against Maddie's throat and tugged on it, slitting it from one end to the other. Maddie stood up, as alarmed as you might expect, and tried to belt her in the face. She stepped back, and as blood squirted all over the place from her neck, Anna shoved the knife up under her chin and tossed her to the ground where she stayed.

'That's more like it,' she said to herself, before she clapped her hands together, turning the TV off and the lights on. She waved her hand over Maddie's dead body. It vanished, leaving behind the same orange stain as before. 'Perfect.'

As the dead body, evidently, couldn't actually be Jon's – or Maddie's, for that matter – Anna had three immediate theories, none of which were very pleasant.

First theory; Jon killed someone and this was their house, before he hid the body and then pretended to be injured himself. Second theory; this *was* Jon's house, and he managed to escape an attack just in time to not fall victim to it. And the third theory; Jon was a zombie.

Anna was secretly interested in the possibility of the third one, but quickly slapped herself across the face when she remembered how, not-so-secretly, she'd been wishing it were aliens, too.

She looked around, wandering through the kitchen and towards the backdoor when she noticed a giant hole in the bottom of it.

'Point of entry,' she said, snapping her fingers. 'Bingo.'

But, upon closer inspection, she realised that it wasn't quite so simple. Getting down on her hands and knees and peering through the makeshift cat flap, Anna noticed large chunks of wood and plastic that'd been strewn about on the patio outside, leading to a similar sized hole in the fence at the top of the garden.

Anna crawled through the hole and picked up one of the wooden shards to take a closer look. 'Huh,' she said, to no one. 'Broken from the inside.'

Something hadn't tried to get in, instead, something had gotten out.

She turned around, quickly, and crawled back into the kitchen through the back door, leading herself through into the bathroom. It was a mess, with blood splattered across the tiles and two holes in the ground, one of which had been filled with cement.

'Jesus.'

She looked down. The trail of blood led out of the bathroom and up the stairs in small, circular blotches. She followed them and came into an empty bedroom.

She heard something, then. Coming from behind her, a high-pitched squeal rattled up the corridor and down the stairs Anna had just climbed. She turned back to face them and heard the light scuttling of feet as they clambered up the staircase.

Oh, shit.

As two spindly black limbs crept up over the top step, pulling the creature they belonged to up after them, Anna froze. For once, perhaps the first time in her life, she was completely still. The monster revealed itself to Anna in the light, and she, internally, described it as any true detective would.

Jesus fucking Christ! What the fucking fuck is that? It's fucking hideous, what the fuck? What? Fucking hell! Fuck!

She'd actually said all those things aloud, too, which confused the creature slightly. Large and crab-like in its appearance, the monster clattered its legs against the carpet as its claws snapped; within the claws themselves were shark-like teeth, and below them was another pair of small gangly arms like that of a T-Rex's, each with long fingers and twisted fingernails.

The creature bent down, a glob of green goo dripping from its mandibles before it charged at Anna.

I fucking knew it, she thought, as death approached. *I knew it'd be aliens.*

Just before it made contact with Anna, a man stepped out from the bedroom she'd just been in, holding a sledgehammer tightly in his grasp as he brought it down on the crab's body. The thick plating on the back of the crab took the full force of the sledgehammer with ease, spraying sparks across the room as if Derek had just struck an anvil.

The crab turned to him, and Anna could see the immediate look of regret across Derek's sweaty face. Without the time to deliver another blow, Derek held the sledgehammer up to defend himself when the crab leapt at him, it's mandibles sinking into the wood about halfway down the handle and snapping the sledgehammer in half. Derek was pinned to the floor. He brought his legs up to kick the creature away, only for it to be back on him an in instant as he tried to crawl towards Anna; towards the only weapon they had.

Anna slapped herself in the face again. She was back in the room, and she had to act fast. This was an actual moment of crisis. Lives were in danger, and this was the chance to prove herself. Picking up the sledgehammer, which was basically the size of a regular hammer by this point, she swung for the crab's front end, bashing one of its claws and taking a small chip out of it.

'Get off him, wankstain!' she yelled, going for another hit.

The creature looked at her from atop Derek's back and screeched as if to simply make fun of how little she could do to stop it, before one of the small T-Rex arms crawled onto Derek's head and three fingers were rammed through the top of his skull. Derek screamed, blood bubbling to the surface of his scalp as the crab-monster rooted around in his brain. The man was trying to speak, but as Anna looked down at him, shaking, she saw Derek's eyes as they liquefied and dribbled out of their sockets.

She brought the hammer down again, which caused the metal head of it to break off, leaving the crab unharmed. She scooped the head up before dashing past the creature and down the stairs as it feasted on Derek's corpse. She thought it'd make her feel better if she looked at the situation more optimistically, as if Derek had chosen to sacrifice himself so that she could live.

It didn't.

She ran for the front door, still clutching the top part of the sledgehammer — the important bit — when the crab-monster barrelled down the staircase and into the living room. She turned back on herself, readying the chunk of metal like it was a shotput.

The crab jumped straight for her, revealing its underside which, as she noted in the brief glimpse she had before action was required of her, lead to a circular mouth-like orifice, filled with more teeth. She threw the hunk of metal towards the crab, striking it directly in the gob and killing all the momentum it had before it dropped to the floor.

It'd eaten the head of the sledgehammer and didn't look too happy about it, either. The crab-monster looked up at her, its claws snapping together.

'Yeah!' she yelled. 'Didn't like that, did ya?'

The crab reared on its back legs and spat the metal head out of its mouth, smashing a nearby window.

'Okay,' said Anna. 'Time to go.'

She pulled the front door open and leapt outside, almost clotheslining herself on the police tape, before she doubled back and went to slam the door in the crab's face, which had already taken to the air again. Being too slow, one of the crab's pointed fingernails clipped the ring finger on Anna's left hand, slicing it open like it was nothing.

'Fucker!' she yelled, slamming the door shut and knocking the crab back into the living room. Anna stumbled backwards and let out a sigh of relief, until she examined her finger once more and found that the top section of flesh was flapping about like a torn-open glove. It stung like hell, and when she blew on it to calm it down, it stung even more.

With the door closed, the creature started bounding into it, putting a large dent in the centre with a single hit. It would buy her time, but not much, as she soon remembered that the back door already had a giant hole in it, and the crab was dead set on getting to its food.

So she ran. She ran straight home, not looking behind her for a second, only thinking one thing the entire way.

It's aliens. It's fucking aliens. I knew it. Maddie is gonna love this.

CHAPTER SEVEN

MADDIE DIDN'T LOVE IT

Maddie had fashioned a chair out of some old pillows and the duvet to Anna's bed so that the man she'd only met fifteen minutes ago could panic to himself in comfort, only for Anna to burst through the door moments later with her finger hanging off.

The man almost fell off his makeshift chair when the door crashed into the wall and a crazy lady came through it.

'You won't fucking believe this!' Anna cried, barrelling into the living room with a pale face. 'You'll never guess what just happened.'

Maddie was stood stock still with her arms crossed, unimpressed. 'I have a new client for you,' she said, as the man gave an awkward wave, wishing he hadn't done. 'I also replaced your lightbulb and... what the bloody hell happened to your hand?'

'Yeah, whatever,' said Anna, not even meeting her client's gaze as she slammed her waist into the cupboard under the sink. She raised her dodgy finger which, by this point, looked as if it'd been crushed in a hydraulic press. 'I'm in a spot of bother.'

'Seems that way,' said Maddie. 'I told you to be careful.'

Anna looked to the top of her head. 'No, you didn't.'

'Well, no,' said Maddie. 'But I thought it would be obvious. What happened?' Maddie took a step closer to Anna, and, upon seeing her finger, recoiled in horror. 'Jesus. You need to go to the hospital.'

'Yeah, yeah, whatever,' Anna replied.

The wound was hurting more than ever, though, and she couldn't deny that. Originally, it was just the horrible feeling of something sharp tearing through her flesh deep enough to strike the bone, but over the course of the walk home it'd evolved into something much worse.

Anna held her finger up to her face and saw how bad it looked. It didn't just look like a layer of bloody meat had been wrapped around a bone, but instead looked like a layer of bloody meat had been wrapped around a bone whilst glowing fucking green. Veins and arteries that she didn't even know existed were all plumped up and throbbing beneath the skin of her finger, and gradually, the green liquid within them started to spread.

'It looks infected,' said Maddie.

'Worse,' Anna replied, letting out a faint sigh, her voice trembling as she did so. 'It's poisoned.'

'Then you *really* need to go to the hospital.'

'I have a plan,' said Anna, using her right hand to reach into one of the cupboards above her head and pull down a metal knife rack. She reached for the biggest handle, pulling free a meat cleaver and slapping it down on the table with a clank. 'Let's do this.'

Maddie wrenched the cleaver away almost instantly like she was confiscating scissors from a child, and refused to give them back. 'You are not cutting off your finger,' she said. 'I forbid it.'

'You're right,' said Anna, clumsily leaning against the worktop. 'You should do it.'

'What? No!'

'It's easy,' Anna went on. 'You've seen Titanic, right?'

Maddie nodded.

'So, you remember that bit where the lady has to chop the bloke out of the handcuffs?'

Maddie nodded.

'I need you to do that, except to my finger. And don't do what that bitch did and close your eyes. It's very important that you don't hit the wrong one.'

'I'm not cutting off your ring finger,' she said. 'It's the finger with that vein that links straight to your heart; it'll kill you.'

'Oh, that's a fucking myth,' Anna said, pointing with her other hand. 'Now get on with it.'

The man, feeling even more unwelcome than he already had done, stood up from his pile of cushions. 'Should I go?' he asked.

'It's fine!' Maddie barked back at him. 'It's fine, you can stay. She isn't always like this.'

'Okay,' said the man, sitting back down, having a strong feeling that she was, in fact, always like this.

'Hurry up,' said Anna, as she slid a chopping board under her finger and splayed it out, away from all her others. 'One quick chop.'

'This is madness,' Maddie replied. 'This is suicide.'

'It's not suicide; at worst it'll be manslaughter. Now fucking cut off my finger.'

'Fine.' Maddie rolled her eyes. 'Fine. I'll do it.'

She lifted the meat cleaver an inch or two above Anna's infected ring finger, and, after hesitating for a moment, she pulled it back and brought it down hard, putting a light crack in the chopping board and nothing else.

'I changed my mind,' Anna said, quickly, having yanked her finger away at the last moment. 'I'll do it. I don't trust you with it.' She took the meat cleaver back.

Maddie sighed into her hands. Grateful, really, that she didn't have to sever somebody's finger after all. She turned her back on the whole thing.

'Okay,' said Anna, struggling to hold the blade steady. 'One quick chop.'

She raised the cleaver above her head, before slamming it down hard just below the knuckle of her finger. She screamed and yelled and called Maddie a rotten bitch and told the guy she didn't even know the name of to go fuck himself, before kicking a massive hole in the cupboard beneath the worktop.

The cleaver hadn't gone right through the finger. It'd struck the bone, only chopping about halfway through it, before failing to make it the rest of the way. She knew that it'd only get worse the longer she waited, so, with another quick chop the cleaver dug itself into the board beneath Anna's severed finger, which is where she left it; embedded.

'Fuck yeah!' Anna yelled in-between bouts of screaming and flailing around. 'I did it!'

There was blood everywhere; spurting out from the stump where her finger should've been, coating the walls and, for a moment, the back of Maddie's head. Maddie turned around. She hated blood, and as she saw Anna smiling gormlessly with it gushing from her hand, she was almost sick.

'What do I do now?' Anna asked. 'I can't just leave it.'

'You go to the hospital,' said Maddie. 'Like I told you to in the first place.'

Anna snapped her fingers – something she could now only do with her right hand – and nodded in Maddie's direction. 'You're right,' she said, turning the knobs on her oven to crank the hob up to full power. 'I need to cauterize the wound.'

'That's not even close to what I said!'

Anna shrugged.

'I really should go,' said the man. 'Coming here was a mistake.'

'Stay there, please!' Maddie yelled. 'Wait your turn.'

'Fucking electric oven,' said Anna, bleeding to death. 'It's gonna take forever to heat up. Maddie, get me a tourniquet.'

'What?'

'Actually, scratch that,' she added, visibly brushing the point away. 'I need you to choke me.'

Gladly, Maddie thought but didn't say. 'Why?'

'It'll cut off the blood flow and I won't bleed to death as quickly.'

'I don't think that's how that works.'

'I'm sure it is.'

'I'm almost positive it isn't.'

'Shut your face and just do it, already,' said Anna, widening her eyes. 'Please?'

Goddammit, Maddie thought. *Why does that always work on me?*

She approached Anna, her choking hands at the ready, when she reached for her throat and squeezed. Maddie knew this wasn't the time – it never was with Anna – but she couldn't shake the idea that it was oddly exciting. It didn't help much, though. Anna's blood still sprayed over the kitchen sink and down the plughole, albeit with less gusto than before, until she pushed Maddie away and gave a half-hearted thumbs up.

'I think I'm good,' Anna mumbled, sounding more and more drunk by the moment before she pressed the bleeding stump against the hob and held it there. The sound of sizzling flesh came first, and then Anna's scream came second, her eyes bolting wide open as the wound was burned shut.

Maddie covered her mouth. It was disgusting to look at, to listen to... to smell.

Eventually, after what felt like an eternity, Anna pulled her hand away from the hob with smoke billowing from her charred finger-stump whilst sweating buckets.

'Is it over?' the man asked, covering his eyes. 'Is it safe to look?'

'I think so,' Maddie replied, covering her mouth. 'Are you okay, Anna?'

She was still standing, which was a good thing, but her balance was starting to go, which wasn't such a good thing. Leaning against the fridge, Anna examined where her finger used to be, and saw that the green poison hadn't spread below the stump, but had instead been contained to the severed finger that sat on the draining board, as she suspected.

Anna reached back into the cupboard and pulled out a jar full of pickled onions in vinegar, before she fished the onions out and tossed them aside, throwing the severed finger into its new home before screwing the lid shut.

'Done,' said Anna, stumbling around. 'Sorted. That's a word, right?'

'I think you should lie down,' said Maddie, reaching out for her. 'You lost a lot of blood. I'll help you to your bed.'

'Nah, I'm fine,' Anna mumbled, almost finding her balance. 'I'll just take a nap here.'

She fell over backwards and bashed her head on the dishwasher on the way to the ground, blacking out before she'd fully reached it.

There was silence.

'So,' said Maddie, turning to the man who, by this point, still hadn't unshielded his eyes. 'That's Anna Pendleton. She's... different. What did you say your name was again?'

'Roberto,' he said, peering between his fingers. 'I think I'm going to leave now if that's okay.'

Without waiting for an answer, he stood up to do just that.

'Wait!' said Maddie, reaching out after him. 'We can help you, I promise. This won't happen again, just please give us a chance.'

He turned back towards her. He looked grumpy, but understood that she really was trying her best. 'I should be going to the police,' he said. 'But, I don't think they'd quite get what's happening. Your friend seems... open-minded.'

'That's one way to put it, yeah.'

'When she came in with her finger looking all busted up, too, it looked similar to what Naomi had.'

'Your wife, right? How so?' Maddie asked. 'If you can bear to wait for just a little while, please come back in the morning, and we'll be able to help you properly. We'll find your wife in no time, I promise. Anna just needs some rest.'

She crouched down beside Anna's unconscious body and pressed the back of her hand against her forehead, before feeling for her pulse, too.

'Yeah,' said Roberto, noting how tenderly Maddie was caring for her friend. 'She left something behind that looks a bit similar.' He sighed. 'And I'll think about it. I have your number, after all.'

'What did she leave behind?' Maddie asked, peering down at the bag by his feet. 'What's in there? It's not another severed appendage, I hope.'

When Roberto saw the innocent smile on her face he looked towards the bag as he thought, carefully, about what was inside of it, before turning back to her. 'You might want to sit down.'

CHAPTER EIGHT

THE OUTSIDER

As she slept off her post-amputation hangover, Anna's mind was all over the bloody place. It'd been a rough day, rougher than most, and her brain had a hard time piecing it all together; so she dreamed.

Anna hated dreaming as a child, and she hated it even more as an adult. At the time, dreams were just a load of nonsensical bollocks that had nothing to do with anything, and simply made something as trivial and wasteful as sleep take longer than it needed to. She just wished that it'd stayed like that after she'd moved away from home, rather than get worse, which is exactly what had happened. Anna wanted to close her eyes when she was tired, and then open them again when she wasn't; simple. The little ad breaks in the middle were not welcome in the slightest, especially when they involved her eyes exploding or her fingernails falling off.

Yes, Anna's dreams were bad, and as she lay in her bed slightly less still than you might expect from a sleeping person, she had one of her worst ones yet.

Her ring finger, the one on her left hand, was still there. She could move it, she could click her fingers with both hands again, and she... well, that was all she actually used that finger for, so that was it, really. Beneath her feet was a jagged, cobblestone pathway where each chunk of rock had been loosely stuck together and, between the gaps, there was nothing, and the same went for everywhere around her. The pathway was the one sign of life – aside from herself – cutting through the light blue abyss that was her nightmare. She could see the wind around her as it rolled about in black swirls, spiralling in on itself, before dissipating and then doing it all over again.

Failing to see the end of the pathway ahead, Anna looked behind her to see if it stretched infinitely in that direction, too. It didn't, and standing on the edge of misshapen rocks, peering down into nothingness, was a man. Anna took a step back. She knew who it was, as there was only one person it could've been.

They were covered in a thick, black mist.

They were the reason she hated going to sleep.

They were the Outsider.

'It's a long way down,' he mumbled, his alien voice shifting with every letter as if each one was being enunciated by a different person. 'You've been away for quite some time. Welcome back, Annie.'

Frozen, Anna's only movement was that of trembling on the spot. The Outsider was the one element of Anna's dreams that'd become familiar to her, so much so that she'd given it a little name of her own. No matter where she was, whether the dream took place in her apartment, under the sea, or even in space, the Outsider was there; not always participating, but always watching.

'Tell me,' he said, peering over his shoulder at her. 'How have you been?'

She didn't reply. Anna wouldn't talk to the man, ever. She knew that if she talked to the man in her dreams it'd make her crazy, and Anna wasn't crazy; absolutely not. Anna blinked and the man at the edge was suddenly facing her, if it could really be called that, as the Outsider himself didn't exactly have much of a face to face her with.

She took another step back, and when a quick jolt of air rushed towards her, the Outsider was right in front of Anna, towering over her as his features constantly mutated and contorted. One moment his eyes were wide and blue, then they were yellow, green, grey, purple, sometimes all at once. Then, just like with Derek's, his eyes would melt out of his head, but unlike Derek's, they would reappear, burst, and then grow back again.

'How have you been?' the Outsider asked again, impatient. 'Solved any more mysteries yet, Annie? Special Annie with the special brain always did like a mystery.'

He smiled so sharply that it tore his cheeks open and blood came dribbling out of them. He knew that she recognised the child-like voice he was using with the last thing he said. He knew how much she hated it.

The Outsider leant forward. 'You lost a lot of blood, Annie,' he whispered in her ear. 'I'm thinking you're mine for a while, now, don't you?'

Fuck off, Anna thought but didn't say. *Don't talk to the dream-man. That'll make you crazy and you are most definitely not crazy.*

She ran like hell in the opposite direction. The ground under her feet was unforgiving, but, she knew that if she fell she might not get back up again. After all, she'd ran along this stone path a dozen times before, and she wasn't looking to fuck it up now. Beside her, the black wind was gliding alongside the pathway until the streaks of darkness flew ahead of her and into the ground, coming together to form a singular, atrocious being.

Six legs, two arms, two claws, and far too many eyes; it was the crab.

Stopping dead in her tracks, Anna was only a couple of feet from the creature as it screeched in her face, its feet clattering against the stones. She spun back, only to see that the Outsider was, still, as close to her as he'd ever been.

'Shit,' she said, before turning around again to see that the Outsider was on that side of her, too, and the crab was nowhere in sight.

'You can't run from me,' he growled, reaching out for Anna's throat with his hand, only for her to smack it away when he got close, pushing him back further than perhaps it should've.

He'd failed, yet again, and he was very pissed off about it.

Anna, doing what she'd always done, ran back the way she came, not worrying about the pathway and how it stopped only a few feet ahead of her. She'd jump off if she had to.

Her hair, which she then realised was no longer tied behind her head in a neat bun, was yanked backwards by the Outsider as he wrapped the locks of ginger around his wrists. She screamed, loud, as some of the hairs were torn from her scalp and she was pulled to her knees.

'You can't keep moving forever,' growled the Outsider, staring down at her. 'And when you stop, I will be there. I am catching up, remember? Remember, Annie?'

Anna pulled back against the Outsider's grip as hard as she could, until a large chunk of her hair came tearing out, blood dripping from her scalp. She crawled away, kicking at the Outsider with her heels until he retired.

'Until next time, Annie,' he said. 'I'm closer than you think.' He snapped his fingers, and as the pathway around Anna crumbled, the nightmare she'd been trapped in did the same.

***

Anna leapt out of bed and almost knocked herself out on the wardrobe as she struggled to get her balance. She was awake, her dream was over, and the Outsider had disappeared along with it; even if its final words rang through her head in a throng of different voices.

Until next time...

Stumbling into her tiny bathroom, groggy, Anna held her left hand up to her face, seeing its full glory in the shine of the bright lamp around her mirror. Thankfully, she was right about the poison, or infection, or whatever it was, as it'd still shown no sign of spreading in the hours that she'd been sleeping. Her hand itself had been bandaged, quite neatly, too, which meant it'd been Maddie's doing. Although, realistically, it couldn't have been anybody else.

Anna didn't have anybody else, and as she looked down at a cup beneath her mirror, seeing two toothbrushes together – one of which had never been touched – the thought lingered in her head, only to be brushed aside shortly after.

She emerged into her living room, almost falling over a nearby wooden chair on the way, before realising that her living room was suddenly home to a wooden chair, which, yes, was very much nearby. The chair was empty. In fact, as far as Anna was aware, the whole apartment was empty aside from herself, which was how she often liked it; if "often" meant "always."

Flicking the lights on, Anna noticed that most of her blood around the kitchen sink had been cleaned away, although, sitting on the worktop, swimming in a jar full of vinegar, was Anna's severed ring finger. She walked closer to it. It'd gone completely green, also turning the vinegar from a clear liquid into a dark, foggier one with lumps in it. Anna thought it was fascinating to look at, though, in the impending-car-crash sort of way, and left it on display beside the kitchen sink.

She looked away from the finger, only to look back towards it, and then away again. She thought she saw it twitch a little in the corner of her eye, but she was also nauseous, dizzy, and seriously needed a wee, so she brushed that thought aside, too.

There's no way it could move, she thought. *That'd be mental. The Crazy Train to What the Fuck-ville.*

Then her mind flashed with images of what she'd seen at Angela's house. The monster, the sinkholes, and the man, Derek, who had his brain turned to soup right in front of her. That monster was still there, or at least she hoped it was, because that'd mean it wasn't scuttling around her apartment building looking for some tasty human brains.

But, what if it'd gotten a taste for her blood? Where did it come from? Were there more of them? What the actual fuck was even going on? Anna asked all these questions aloud, to herself, as she cranked open the one and only set of blinds in the living room. The darkness from the early-morning winter made her feel uneasy, so she closed them again; but not before spotting a note left on the worktop. She looked at it, seeing nothing more than a jumble of random letters and scrawlings until she realised that she was just trying to read it upside down.

Sitting down on the floor beside the wooden chair, Anna read the note to herself.

I let myself out, it read, in Maddie's handwriting. *Your new client is giving you the benefit of the doubt after last night's display, so be ready for about ten in the morning and let's see how we can help him. This could be huge,* the note went on. *This is an actual, serious mystery. I know how you've always wanted one of those. See you soon x.*

Anna scrunched the note up and tossed it across the room. It was half past five, which gave her plenty of time to shower, get dressed, and even go back to bed. She didn't do the last one, of course, having another cup of her sugar-filled drink that vaguely resembled a cup of tea as she fiddled about with her hair, her face, and just about everything, really; whatever she could to avoid sitting still or relaxing in any way.

My hair, she thought, the pain of having it torn out suddenly returning at the mere thought of it. *My bloody hair.*

She rushed back into the bathroom and looked at herself in the mirror again. It was all still there, as far as she could tell, hanging a few inches below her shoulders. It was long, but, until she had that dream, she'd never really considered it to be "too long" before. She ran her hands through it again, and as she did, a few dozen hairs fell out and drifted into the sink. Looking down at them, she reached for the scissors.

Until next time... she heard, again, before she hacked away at her hair until the sun came up. *I'm closer than you think.*

CHAPTER NINE

AN ACTUAL, SERIOUS MYSTERY

'What happened to your hair?' was Maddie's first question, before Anna yanked her into her apartment and slammed the door. 'It looks like a pixie cut but you gave up halfway through.'

'There's a lot of shit happening that we need to talk about,' Anna replied, peering over Maddie's shoulder. 'Where's that guy?'

'I said he'd be here at ten.'

'It is ten, isn't it?'

'Nope.'

'Then why are you here?'

'Because I got here early.'

'Oh,' said Anna. 'Why?'

'Does it matter?' Maddie replied.

'Not really.'

'Cool, now, what did you need to tell me?'

'I found something last night when I visited that address,' Anna said, looking down at her feet, and then up again. 'The aliens are here.'

There was a moment of silence, and then Maddie burst out laughing until she noticed that Anna didn't, and decided to stop. 'Oh, no, you're serious.'

'Very.'

'Aliens aren't real, Anna. I think you need to go back to bed; get some more sleep,' said Maddie, taking her phone out. 'I'll ring your client and tell him that we're cancelling so you can...'

'No!' Anna interrupted Maddie by grabbing ahold of her face and staring into her eyes, looking absolutely mental and knocking her phone across the room. 'Aliens!' she yelled. 'Aliens are real. There are aliens here, just like I said. Aliens, aliens, aliens!'

'Stop saying that.'

'Aliens, Madeleine. Real, actual aliens.'

There was a pause.

'Can you let go of my face, please?' asked Maddie.

She did.

'Thanks,' Maddie added, strolling across the room to pick her phone up off the floor, noticing a giant crack across the screen that wasn't there a few minutes ago. 'Unbelievable.'

'I know. It sounds crazy.'

'Not that, jackass. You busted my phone when you smacked it across the room.'

'Aliens are here, Maddie. We don't have time to worry about stuff like that.'

'So you keep saying, but you haven't actually told me anything other than the fact that there are aliens, and that, surprisingly, they are here.'

Anna raised her left hand and slapped it about in Maddie's face. 'One of the bastards did this to my finger.'

'No,' said Maddie. '*You* did that to your finger.'

'Well, yes, but I did it because of the aliens.'

'The aliens made you cut off your finger?'

'In a way, yes.'

'How? Mind control?'

'Mind control? That's absurd, Maddie. Mind control isn't real.'

Maddie's head slammed into her palms. 'I'm going to scream,' she whispered to herself.

'I went to that house, yeah,' Anna went on, 'with the address from that guy...'

'Which you stole.'

'Which I stole, yes. And you'll never guess what.'

'You found aliens?'

'Stranger than that. It wasn't actually his house.'

Maddie glanced off to the side as if she were looking into a camera on some trashy, insane reality television show, in which she was the idiot being pranked. 'Then who's was it?'

'Not sure, but, there was blood everywhere, and, well, a dead body or two after I left.'

'Dead bodies?' said Maddie. 'Why didn't you call anyone?'

'Who would I call?'

'The police?'

'Nah, sod them. That's not the important part, anyway.'

'Right.'

'Y'know those sinkholes that keep popping up?'

'Yeah. They're just some natural thing where the water erodes the ground to collapse the earth or something.'

'No,' Anna replied. 'It's because of...'

'Aliens, right? Good lord, you're actually making me sound like the intelligent one, you know. Coffee?'

'How would you explain them, then?'

'With the explanation I just gave you. Or Google it, if you have to. I'm sure Wikipedia will tell you in five seconds.'

'There'd be nothing about aliens on there.'

'Because aliens aren't real. Are you having a coffee, or not?'

'Yes, please. Nine sugars, no milk.'

'Nine sugars...' Maddie whispered to herself, as she turned away and flicked the kettle on, her body suddenly jolting backwards once she spotted the severed finger, still in the jar by the sink. 'That's so disgusting.'

'My coffee?' called Anna, as she paced around the other side of the room.

'No, your finger. Why did you have to keep it?'

'I dunno. It might come in handy.'

'You're cra—' she stopped herself. 'You're weird.'

'Why isn't that guy here yet?' said Anna. 'He's late.'

'It's not ten yet,' Maddie replied. 'He'll be here at ten.'

'It's gotta be ten by now.'

'It's ten to ten.'

'Yeah, that's basically ten. That's actually two tens so I'd argue that it's more like ten 'o' clock than ten 'o' clock is, if you actually think about it.'

'That doesn't make any sense, Anna,' said Maddie, as she poured the boiling water into the mugs, just in time for someone to knock on the door. 'Never mind, that'll probably be him.'

'For fuck sake. I have a doorbell. Why does nobody ring the damn doorbell? What's the point, man?' Anna stomped over to the door to answer it.

Maddie placed the kettle back into its charger. 'Are you going to be okay?' she asked. 'We can always cancel it, still. You seem off. Well, you always seem off, but this is a whole new kind of off.'

'Yeah, fine, whatever,' said Anna, scratching at her scalp. 'Living the dream.'

'A nightmare, more like.'

Anna shuddered. 'I'm fine,' she said, slowing down for just a moment. 'Don't worry.'

'One last thing...'

'What?'

'Please, for the love of god, don't mention anything about aliens.'

She thought about it, perhaps for longer than she should have. 'Fine, whatever. No aliens, you have my word.'

***

'So,' said Anna, as her client – dressed in a suit that was probably more expensive than Anna's entire apartment – sat on the flimsy wooden chair in her living room, of which she still didn't have a bloody clue how it got there. 'Tell us what happened.'

'Well,' said Roberto, his throat clicking as he swallowed. 'I was out walking with my wife, Naomi, and...'

'Okay,' said Anna, 'when I said tell us what happened, I don't mean tell us, like, the whole thing; just the important bits.'

Maddie kicked her in the side of the leg. 'Behave,' she whispered.

'Oh, right,' said Roberto, slipping a handkerchief out of his breast pocket and wiping his forehead with it. 'Of course. It was dark and, I turned my back on her for a second, then when I looked back she was gone.'

'Interesting,' Anna nodded. 'Have you considered that it might've been al...'

Maddie kicked her in the leg again.

'A sudden fall,' Anna corrected herself. 'Perhaps she slipped and hurt herself and you didn't notice.'

'Well, I thought that at first,' Roberto went on. 'But, she started to call me for help.'

'And did you?'

'Did I what?'

'Help her.'

'Yes, of course I did.'

'Well, you tried to, anyway.'

'I'm sorry?'

'Okay, I'll take over from here,' said Maddie, barging Anna out of the way. 'What happened next?'

Roberto looked at Maddie, before his eyes shifted to Anna, and then back again. 'There's a storm drain underneath the south bridge,' he went on. 'Something pulled her in, and, that was it. She was gone. I haven't heard from her since. Her family's worried sick, and of course, I'm getting the blame for it, which is fair enough I guess, but, what could I do? I'm worried, too.'

Anna eye's drifted downwards, looking beneath Roberto's feet. 'What's in the bag?' she asked.

'I'll show you,' he replied, taking the bag up onto his lap and unzipping it.

'Oh, I can't watch this,' said Maddie, looking away. 'I've seen this once already.'

'Pussy,' said Anna. 'Surely it can't be that bad...'

He took out Naomi's severed hand in a little plastic sand-wich bag and dangled it in front of Anna's face.

'Okay,' she said, sucking her lips in. 'Why the hell have you got that? Is it a souvenir, or something?'

'It was the only part of her left.'

Anna crept closer to the bag, and subsequently Roberto, as he looked more uncomfortable by the second. 'Can I hold it?'

Roberto went to unzip the bag.

'I meant the bag, too, dummy,' she added, snatching it away from him. 'It's a bit green, don't you think?' She looked over to her jar-finger by the kitchen sink, and then to the hand. 'Wait here,' she said, tossing the bag at Roberto and almost slapping him in the face with it before she rushed over to the kitchen area.

'They do look pretty similar,' said Maddie, struggling to keep her breakfast in. 'It might just be because it's started rotting, though.'

'Flesh doesn't rot like that, silly,' said Anna, as if it were obvious. 'This is different. It's gotta be...'

'Don't say it.' Maddie raised a finger to silence her. 'I don't want you dropping the A-bomb now.'

'Dropping the A-bomb?' Anna asked. 'Did you just make that up?'

There was a pause.

'I might've done.'

'Okay,' said Anna, turning her attention back to Roberto. 'Sorry, Roger, but your wife was murdered by aliens.'

'Anna!'

'Oh, my bad, sorry. I meant *Roberto*, yes. *Roberto*, your wife was murdered by aliens.' Anna turned to Maddie. 'Better?'

Maddie said nothing.

'What do you mean?' asked Roberto, standing up. 'What are you talking about?'

'Ignore her,' said Maddie. 'She's clearly still a bit delusional after the amputation. I'm sorry for wasting your time.'

'I'm not delusional!' Anna yelled, stopping the room dead. 'I'm right about this. I've seen them. I've seen the aliens, they're real.'

'Aliens?' asked Roberto. 'Here, in England?'

'Aliens, here in England,' Anna confirmed.

'What do these aliens even look like?' Maddie asked.

'Okay. This is gonna sound weird...'

'The whole thing has sounded pretty weird so far,' said Maddie. 'You might as well keep going with it.'

'They're like these big crab things with little dinosaur arms and a weird, toothy butt underneath.'

'A toothy-what?'

'Doesn't matter. The point is that they're burrowing under the ground, creating little sinkholes all over the place and eating people. It's mental.' Anna turned to Roberto. 'Where did you say it happened again?'

'J—Just below the south bridge,' he said. 'The storm drain is beneath it, beside the lake.'

'Good to know,' said Anna, snapping the fingers on the right hand, and failing to do so on her left before heading for the door. 'I'll head there now, and call you when I find something.'

She opened the door, only for Maddie to step in the way and slam it closed again, keeping her hand over the doorknob. 'We're going with you,' she said. 'I want to see these things for myself.'

'No, you really don't,' Anna replied, knocking her hand away. 'I'm going on my own. I'll be fine.'

'I don't believe you. The last time you went somewhere on your own, which I would like to remind you was incredibly recently, you lost a finger.'

'It won't happen again.'

'Because we're going to be there,' said Maddie, turning to Roberto. 'Get your things,' she went on. 'We have work to do.' She faced Anna. 'You're not well. You say and do some weird stuff on the daily, I get that, but you're losing it. You need to rest.'

'I'm fine,' Anna snarled, grabbing Maddie by the shoulders. 'There is nothing wrong with me, okay? I need the money, that's all,' she said, taking out Jon's penniless debit card, which she stole, before flinging it across the room like a Frisbee. 'And I want this job to be done properly.'

'Then let us help you,' said Maddie, looking deep into her eyes. 'Please.'

Anna's eyes looked almost everywhere but towards the woman talking to her, until she met her gaze, and smiled. 'Okay,' she said. 'But this is the only time.'

'Sure,' Maddie replied. 'I'll take it.'

'I'm sorry if this ruins the moment,' came Roberto's timid voice from across the room, 'but could I quickly use your bathroom?'

'First door on the left,' said Anna, not taking her eyes off of Maddie. 'Knock yourself out.'

He did, albeit only figuratively, which Anna found a tad disappointing.

'So, what are we going to do if we see these things?' Maddie asked.

'I dunno,' Anna replied, sliding over to the kitchen cupboards. 'Scream, probably.'

'Okay, but, I meant in a more productive sense. What are we going to do?'

Anna grabbed the drawer beside her waist and yanked the entire thing out, before hoisting onto the counter and pouring the contents out onto the worktop. 'I don't know why I did that,' she said, staring at piles and piles of spoons, butter knives, and plastic cutlery. 'These won't be even slightly useful.'

'Your knives are in the cupboard above your head,' Maddie replied, thankful that she wasn't letting Anna out of her sight again.

What the hell has gotten into her?

'Here we are!' Anna declared, tossing a serrated bread knife across the room where it clattered across the floor. 'Think fast.'

'You're supposed to say that before you throw it, Anna. And you shouldn't be throwing knives in the first place.'

'Yeah, yeah, whatever,' she replied. 'These should do. If we see one of those things, then, I dunno, give it a stab. Their armour is really thick, too, so it's best to go for the bit where the butt-teeth are.'

'The underside?'

'Yeah, that bit.'

The toilet behind them loudly flushed and Roberto came wandering out, looking as confused as ever as the two women in front of him were brandishing big, deadly weapons.

'Okay,' said Maddie, slipping the knife into her purse. 'Are we ready?'

Anna spun the cleaver around on one of the fingers before dumping it into her rucksack along with a small LED flashlight and bottle of water. 'Ready.'

'Do I get anything?' Roberto asked.

'Ah, yes, your one is the best,' said Anna, before handing him something lightweight and metallic.

It was a bottle opener.

'Oh,' he said, forcing a smile. 'It's great. Thanks.'

'Sweet. Let's go and find us some giant crab-looking toothy butt aliens!'

'We're not calling them that,' said Maddie. 'I forbid it.'

'Oh?' Anna asked. 'What would you call 'em?'

CHAPTER TEN

COLLAPSE

Geoffrey Tilbrook, part-time teacher and full-time couch potato, was inside his house making his own personal variation of beans on toast when the ground opened up underneath him and swallowed his entire house.

It didn't happen right away, although, as Geoff felt some rumblings beneath his feet he immediately felt uneasy. He knew that sinkholes were a thing, and, as a man living alone – aside from a pet goldfish which was the last one standing out of a group of six – he knew it'd be unlikely that anyone would be there to help him if he were to get caught in one. On this day in particular, though, it didn't really matter.

There was nothing he could do.

As Geoff finished scattering a layer of cheese across the beans that – were he to eat them at their initial temperature – would probably burn his entire face right off of his head, he felt the ground shake. After getting food poisoning in college one whole time, Geoff always followed the mantra of "if it's burnt, it's not undercooked" and proceeded to crucify every meal until it looked absolutely nothing like what was displayed on the packet. The fact that baked beans wouldn't give him food poisoning regardless of how he cooked them wasn't something he really cared about, either.

He wanted to be safe, rather than sorry, and he most definitely wasn't looking to die anytime soon.

Whilst the ground shook, Geoff looked out of the window to see if there was a nearby reason for the disturbance, but found himself just staring at his own reflection as it was the middle of the night and very bloody dark, indeed. He sat down at his sofa, pretended nothing was out of the ordinary, and started eating.

The rumbling didn't stop; if anything, it got louder, and closer, so much so that one of his workbooks fell off the shelf behind him and bashed him on the back of the head, knocking his glasses into his dinner.

Geoff leapt up. His vision was blurry, his ears were ringing, and there were beans all over the damn place.

The ground shook again, and, thinking it was an earthquake or something more, Geoff ran between the doorframe to his kitchen and cowered there. More books came flying off the shelf and crashing onto the carpet, framed pictures tore holes in the wallpaper as they slid off their brackets and windows were blown out; spraying glass.

Then it all went silent. There was nothing, just the sound of Geoff's heart pounding in his chest and forcing blood into his brain. He looked at the ground, and just as he stood up, relieved that it was all over, the ground tore open beneath his feet and he – along with his house and everything that he ever cared about – fell into the darkness below.

That's when it was really all over, or, it would've been if it weren't for one man.

Everything went black, and as Geoff stared at the inside of his eyelids, they were forced open. At first glance, he thought there was nothing around him except darkness, but when he looked down he saw a jagged, cobblestone pathway beneath his feet.

'What's happening?' he said, still without his glasses. 'Am I dead?'

'Almost,' replied a voice, followed by a growl that endlessly shifted in pitch until it was over. 'But you don't have to be.'

Oh god, Geoff thought. *That can't be good.*

A bright light burst through his blurred vision, revealing a shadowy figure ahead of him. It reached out, slowly, as if it were getting ready to strike. Geoff's mind went rampant. What were they going to do to him? Snap his neck? Tear his head off? Pull his eyes out and violate the sockets?

Okay, he thought to himself. *Probably not that last one.*

Geoff braced his whole body regardless, ready for death to come, for real this time, only to have his glasses lightly pushed onto his nose. His sight was back, and when he saw the man standing opposite him – his face smashed into a pulp, twisting this way and that – he wished that he hadn't.

'The old man,' the stranger said. 'Years spent wasting away and without anything meaningful to show for it.'

'Where am I?' he asked. 'What's going on?'

'I saved your life,' said the stranger, looking Geoff up and down with his arms crossed. 'Do you trust me?'

'I... I don't know what's happening.' Geoff took a few steps back. 'I'm just gonna go. Thanks for the help.' He turned around, only for the stranger to pop up right in front of his face again. Geoff yelped and fell over backwards, smacking his head on the pavement. 'Christ!'

'No, no, no,' said the stranger, his voice slow and almost seductive; assuming Geoff was into nutters, which wasn't important at that moment in time. 'I helped you, and now, you're going to do something for me.'

'What?' Geoff mumbled. 'No.'

There was a pause.

'Did you just say no to me?' asked the stranger.

Geoff went to say it again but stopped himself. He tried to sit up, only for the figure ahead of him to dart forwards and kick him in the chest, knocking him to the ground again. 'I helped you,' said the stranger. 'I don't like it when people don't return the favour. I always find those who owe me something, and you owe me. Remember?'

'Y-Yeah, yes, of course,' said Geoff, nodding, unsure if he meant it. 'What do you need?'

That was exactly what the stranger wanted to hear, making him flash a jagged-toothed smile. 'Good,' he growled, before he gently ran his hand up Geoff's chest.

Oh shit, thought Geoff. *This is not what I had in mind.*

Thankfully, neither did the stranger, as he reached into Geoff's jacket pocket and placed something inside, giving it a light tap. 'This will help you get out of the worm,' said the stranger. 'Don't let me down.'

'Worm?' Geoff asked, still frozen to the spot. 'What worm? What are you talking about?'

The stranger leant closer to Geoff's ear and whispered three words into it, sending his mind into a frenzy. His eyes glazed over and his heart-rate shot through the roof as he felt as if he were falling, again, just as he had before the stranger had caught him.

He woke up a few hours later. He didn't know where he was, but he sure as hell wasn't in his house anymore. The walls were pink, and, upon closer inspection, moving ever so slightly; like they were alive. The air was thick and humid, and as Geoff took out his phone to use the flashlight, something fell into his lap along with it.

He fumbled around for a moment, eventually snagging a thin piece of card that he shone his flashlight over, reading what looked like a business card with an email address, a Twitter handle, and a link to something called a "subreddit."

What the hell is that? Geoff thought, which is when he was promptly reminded he was pushing fifty.

The card didn't make much sense, not at first, anyway, until the words spoken by the stranger echoed clearly in his mind, as if he were hearing them again anew, over and over again in a different voice each time.

Find Anna Pendleton, the voice had said; a voice belonging to the Outsider.

CHAPTER ELEVEN

SEWER GREMLIN

'It smells like butt in here,' said Anna, leaning into the storm drain as she attempted to tie her hair behind her head, before realising she didn't have enough and giving up entirely. 'We ready, gang? We're gonna catch ourselves a crab-monster.'

'That name isn't much better than the last one,' said Maddie, standing beside Roberto, firmly outside of the storm drain. 'Not that it matters, anyway.'

'We aren't actually going to try and fight one, are we?' Roberto asked, fumbling with his tie. 'I'm not much of a fighter and we really shouldn't be here after dark.'

'Yeah, how long is this gonna take?'

'Holy shit,' said Anna, holding her hands up. 'You don't get to complain the whole time we're here, or I'll turn around and we'll go right back home again. Got it?'

Maddie and Roberto nodded.

'Good,' said Anna, scratching at her skin. 'Just gimme a moment. I need to work something out.'

Anna took a step back into the clearing, under the South Bridge, before closing her eyes. Meanwhile, Roberto watched with a great degree of confusion as she then proceeded to flail her arms around like a lunatic, all while Maddie tried not to laugh.

'What is she doing?' Roberto asked, with genuine concern. 'Is she okay?'

'She's fine,' Maddie replied. 'She always does this. She likes to recreate the scene of the crime in her head, so to speak. Helps her visualize what might've happened so she can find a solution.'

'Oh,' said Roberto, looking at Anna, before going back to Maddie. 'Does it work?'

'I have no idea.'

To Anna, the sun had already gone down, and as she waved the moon upwards into the sky, she felt a creeping darkness emerge from the storm drain. She crouched down, reaching out into the black to find Maddie's body. She was flailing and struggling as something tore at her leg. Anna took out her phone, the glow from its flashlight glistening off of the crab-monster as it sunk its claws into Maddie's leg.

Reaching out, Anna grabbed Maddie by the hand and tried to pull her to safety, but the opposing force was too much for Maddie's wrist to handle, and so her muscles tore and her tendons split, causing Anna to tumble backwards with a severed hand held tightly in her own.

'Okay,' said Roberto. 'She's now lying on the floor for some reason?'

'She does that,' said Maddie, the real one. 'She probably just imagined me dying again.'

'Does she often do that, too?'

'All the damn time.'

'FUCK!' Anna yelled, leaping up into the air as the sun reappeared in the sky and Maddie's fake corpse vanished. 'That doesn't make sense.'

'You found something?' Maddie asked, arms crossed.

Anna's eyes locked onto Roberto, who backed away ever so slightly, looking rather worried indeed.

'Come 'ere,' said Anna, charging over to him. 'Let me try something.' She grabbed ahold of Roberto's arm and pulled, almost toppling him. 'How strong are you?'

'Oh,' Roberto replied. 'I—'

'C'mon, I haven't got all day. How strong are you? Strong enough to pull someone's hand off?'

'Well, I don't know, I...'

'You said her hand came off in yours, yeah? You tried to hold onto her, to pull her to safety and BAM!'

Everyone jumped.

'Jesus, Anna,' said Maddie, clutching her chest. 'Don't do that.'

'Sorry,' she replied. 'But, here's the thing, I'm saying that the alien could've easily dragged you into the drain with it.'

'So?'

'So, why didn't it?' Anna met Roberto's gaze again. 'And there's no way your scrawny arse could've fought against that thing. I mean, look at you.'

'Anna!' Maddie called out.

'Now, look, gimme your hand,' Anna said to Roberto, causing him to hold his arm outright, scared of what she might do to it.

'No, your other hand.'

He raised the other arm, equally as confused.

'Jesus, fuck, I mean the one in the bag.'

'Oh,' said Roberto. 'Sorry.'

He reached into his bag and pulled out his wife's severed, rotting hand, and tossed it over.

'Thank you,' she said, looking it all over. 'See, look at the way the wrist is severed,' she went on, shoving it right in their faces.

'I'd rather not,' Maddie replied.

'The wrist has been cut away, not torn. The wound is far too clean. The thing that killed your wife left the hand on purpose, it must've done.'

'K-Killed?' Roberto stuttered.

'Be sensitive, Anna,' said Maddie. 'We talked about this.'

'Yeah, yeah, whatever. Point is...'

'The monster wasn't willing to risk losing one victim for two.'

'Exactly!' Anna snapped, clicking her fingers all around her head. 'It needed your wife for something, which means...'

'She might still be alive?' said Roberto.

There was a pause.

'Well...' said Anna, drawing out all the letters for far too long, only to look over and see Maddie frowning. 'Oh, yeah, totally. She might very well be alive, yes.' Anna met Maddie's gaze. 'How was that? Was that okay?'

Another pause.

'Doesn't matter,' Anna went on. 'Basically, we're gonna pop into the storm drain, have a quick root around for the crab thingy, and try and find your wife's body.'

More stares.

'Your wife's very-much-alive body,' she went on, smiling.

The three of them, somewhat satisfied, stood at the entrance to the storm drain and peered into the darkness with Anna using her handheld flashlight to light up the inside.

'Right,' she said, flicking her fringe from her face. 'Let's get a wiggle on.'

***

The ground squelched under Anna's boots as she, taking the lead, led the trio further into the dark. With little room to move around, Maddie was at the back of the queue, whilst Roberto lingered somewhere in the middle. Roberto said he felt safer there, Anna said it was because he was a pussy, and Maddie said it was because she only gave him a bottle opener to defend himself.

They were all correct, to some degree.

Pushing onward, Anna came to a slope that was trickling water downwards into a much larger area.

'Oh, shit,' she said.

'What?' Roberto asked. 'Is it bad?'

'Only one way to find out.'

Anna leapt forward onto the slope as if getting ready to sail down a water slide, letting out a cheer, only to immediately come to a stop after moving less than an inch down the pipe, doing little more than making her trousers damp.

'Well, that was shit,' said Anna. 'Sorry, as you were.'

'What happened?' asked Roberto.

'She's being an idiot, again,' Maddie replied.

'Fuck off,' said Anna, and the three continued on their way.

After wandering down the slope the trio were allowed more breathing room as they emerged in a large, but equally as dark part of the sewer system. It was a large, circular area that stretched several feet above and below where they were. A ring of dim lights were dotted evenly around the inside, too, showing off the sheer size of the place.

Anna came to a railing, which had become rusted and clammy, before leaning over it.

'Can't see anything,' said Anna. 'Too dark.'

'Because you're not using your bloody flashlight,' Maddie replied.

'Oh yeah,' said Anna, flicking it on. 'Whatever.'

The light didn't make it far before it bounced off of something. Sharing a similar dark, damp aesthetic as the rest of the place, Anna assumed that it was just the next level down, but the raw and rusted look of the platform still made her feel uneasy as it glistened back at her. There were ridges along it, too. Some were thick and bulbous, some were sharp and jagged, and overall it looked like something you absolutely should not – under any circumstances – be stepping foot onto.

'Let's hop down there,' Anna said, tapping on the railing, before Maddie leapt over it, falling all the way to the ground and breaking her legs on the bottom.

'Everything okay?' Maddie asked, the real one, as she stood right next to her. 'Did you say we should jump down?'

'Erm...' Anna met her gaze. 'Maybe we should find a ladder first.'

Looking around, neither Anna nor Maddie had noticed that Roberto wasn't exactly participating like the rest of them were. Anna had almost instantly forgotten that he existed when she wasn't looking at him, and Maddie was too distracted by Anna as she flailed around, slapped herself in the face a few times to concentrate, and crawled along the floor like some kind of goblin.

Goddammit, Maddie thought. *What the hell do you see in her?*

That's when Anna leapt up and grabbed Maddie by the face. 'I've found a way,' she said, eagerly. 'Progress! It's exciting! Right? Isn't it exciting? Maddie?'

She looked deep into Anna's eyes, seeing how passionate she was about all this and how beautiful she looked in the light – no matter how low – and sighed.

'It sure is,' said Maddie, smiling. 'Let's go.'

Roberto made himself known, then.

'Guys?' he said, fumbling with the light on his phone. 'I think I've found something.'

'Yeah, yeah, whatever,' said Anna, turning away from him. 'What is it?'

'What did you say those... aliens... looked like?' His voice was high pitched, this time. He was concerned; afraid.

'They're like these big crab things with little dinosaur arms,' she said, repeating herself as if it were obvious. 'And a weird, toothy butt underneath. Why?'

'Oh,' said Roberto. 'So, a bit like that, then?'

Everyone's eyes darted towards where Roberto was pointing his flashlight, showing a six-legged monster with a thick, shiny carapace as it slowly crept down the wall above them.

'What?' asked Maddie. 'What the hell?'

'Oh, shit!' said Anna, excitedly. 'That's the one.'

'I'm sorry, what?' Maddie asked again. 'That thing is real?'

'Yeah, of course it is, I told you this earlier.' Anna cheered. 'Fuck yeah, dude. It's the crabby butt-tooth aliens.'

'We are still so not calling them that,' Maddie's voice quivered.

'Okay!' barked Roberto, fumbling for his bottle opener. 'This is hardly the time!'

The crab's claws dug themselves into the concrete wall, spraying dust into Roberto's eyes, before it looked up and raised one of its crooked fingers, pointing at Anna.

'Hey,' she said. 'I think it remembers me.'

It screeched in her face and lunged straight for her, claws snapping together, ready to tear her to pieces. She stared at it, like an idiot, until she felt Maddie wrap her arms around her waist and throw her out of the way. The crab carried on going, and in an attempt to save her friend, Maddie failed to fully get out of the way herself, sending her back into the railing and straight through it as a blunt section of claw hit her square in the face.

Tumbling off the edge, Maddie hit the ground with her back and, surprisingly, found it to be quite a comfortable landing as if she'd fallen onto a floor-sized mattress. A very damp and gross smelling floor-sized mattress.

'Maddie!' Anna yelled. 'Are you okay?'

'CHRIST!' Maddie yelled back, wiping the blood from her forehead. 'That'll leave a bruise.'

'Is it safe to come down?'

'I think so,' said Maddie, before she sat upright and found herself face to face with the crab-monster. 'OH SHIT!'

As it roared in her face she rolled to the side and stood up, struggling to find her balance on whatever it was she was now standing on.

What is this? Maddie thought. *It feels like a bouncy castle.*

She didn't have time to ponder it further as the crab was ready to make another strike. Then a scream echoed from above.

'LOOK OUT BELOW!'

It was Anna, yelling before she came crashing down butt-first onto the crab. The impact wedged it an inch or two into the floor, pissing off the crab a little bit more, and really hurting her backside. She stood upright and felt her boots sink into the ground when she put her weight on it.

'What the fuck is this shit?' she said. 'It's all spongey.'

'This is no time to discuss the details of the floor,' Maddie barked. 'Kill that bloody thing.'

Roberto was still up above, looking down into the darkness as he thought about what to do.

Don't get involved, he thought. *This isn't your place. Leave them to it. They know what they're doing.*

So, he did, getting distracted by something off to the side.

Looking back towards the crab, Anna noticed that it'd started to dig its way out of the ground, ripping and tearing through the area beneath itself.

'Oh, no you don't!' said Anna, as she took out her meat cleaver and struck it against the crab's carapace.

A few sparks flew, but aside from that, it was unharmed.

'Okay, that sucked.'

'Hit it again!' said Maddie. 'Go for the weak spots!'

'What weak spots?'

'Find the weak spots!'

'How am I supposed to do that?'

'Oh, for Christ's sake.' Maddie stood up, taking out her serrated bread knife with a flourish. 'Like this!'

The crab had almost broken free, before Maddie jammed the blade into its face, splitting an eyeball wide open. It screamed before she stabbed it again and again, going for the same place. By the time it'd broken free it only had one eye left, and as it stumbled around, dazed, Maddie yanked the cleaver from Anna's grasp and chopped its little T-rex arms off, before jamming the cleaver into its underbelly and splitting it open.

Its blood spilt out onto the ground, and its twitching claws came to a halt as its life ended.

'Bloody hell,' said Anna, as Maddie was on her knees, panting. 'You alright?'

She took a deep breath. 'All good,' she said, with a thumbs up. 'I think I needed that.'

'Weirdo,' thought Anna, before something slapped against the ground beside her.

It was a bottle opener.

'Oh, thanks for the help!' Anna called up, brimming with sarcasm. 'Nice to see that this was a fucking team effort. Twat.'

Roberto was nowhere to be seen, and, without his weapon, that wasn't good.

Maddie looked up, face still brimming with sweat, and became a tad concerned. 'Is he alright?' she asked. 'Maybe we should go and check on him.'

'Roger'll be fine,' she said, jumping up and down on the soft floor as if it were a trampoline. 'What is this stuff?'

Maddie frowned. 'I'm going to check on him,' she said. 'You're welcome to join me.'

'Yeah, yeah, whatever,' said Anna, taking out her flashlight and shining it along the ground.

It was strange to look at. It was stiff and coarse at first, like soft concrete, but had a rubbery texture and looked to be covered with little lumps, all varying in size and full of liquid.

'How bizarre,' she said, talking to nobody. She got on her knees, stuck out her tongue, and licked the ground. 'Hmm. Tastes like metal.'

Her light glided further across the ground, bouncing rays off of the dead crab's armoured back, and illuminating the hole it'd made after Anna landed on it arse-first. The hole was pinkish and tender, and as Anna looked at it closely she saw that it began to fill itself in. After a few seconds the sides of the wound pinched itself closed, and it was as if the hole hadn't even been there in the first place.

'Wound,' Anna whispered, as, to her, that was the only way she could see to describe it. 'That can't be good.'

The ground rumbled beneath her feet, slowly at first, but as rumbling wasn't something the ground would often do unless it were for a bad reason, she backed towards the ladder; slowly.

'Easy, now,' she said, arms out as if she was taming a creature, and that creature was the floor. 'Take it easy.'

More rumbles. Harsher rumbles. Louder rumbles.

'I don't want any trouble,' she said, reaching out behind her for the cold, wet feeling of the ladder's rungs. 'I'm just going to go, now. Okay?'

The ground roared back with a thick, harsh growl that shook the entire sewage system; echoing upwards. Anna popped the flashlight in between her teeth and threw herself onto the ladder, just as the ground disappeared beneath her feet.

It was well and truly alive.

Flowing away like a river made of flesh and blood, the thing Anna had been standing on rushed away in an instant, groaning as it did so, until Anna was left dangling off of a ladder that'd been broken just beneath her feet. When she looked over her shoulder and down into the darkness, she thought that it might as well have been infinite, and since the idea of falling a really bloody long way didn't seem all that appealing to Anna, she shot up the ladder as quick as she could, throwing herself onto the metal catwalk above.

'Giant crab?' she whispered to herself. 'No. Too soft.' She licked her lips and slapped herself in the face. 'Idiot. Is that what a crab tastes like? I should've had a bite of that dead one.'

The dead one, assuming it hadn't gotten pulled away when the floor decided to go for a walk, was still down there, somewhere. She just needed to find it, but now wasn't the time, as she heard shuffling come from behind her, turning to face it as soon as it were nearby.

It was Roberto, and Maddie, carrying a body.

'What's this?' Anna asked, to Maddie, who was holding Naomi's legs.

'He found her,' she replied. 'She's still breathing.'

'Oh, fuck yeah,' said Anna, as her eyes went to a puffy-eyed Roberto, holding her upper half, before going down to

Naomi's hand, and then across to her stump where the other one used to be. 'Wait, I have so many questions.'

'Ask them later.'

There was a pause as her eyes drifted over to the bag that'd slipped off of Roberto's shoulder, with Naomi's hand still inside.

'I wonder if she'll want that back,' Anna said. 'Is that a thing? Do people do that with limbs?'

'Shut up, Anna,' Maddie said, as she wiggled her way back into the storm drain. 'We're going to the hospital.'

'Okay,' Anna called after. 'I'll catch up!'

She turned back towards the pit and stared down into it, before reaching into her bag, pulling out a water bottle, and tossing it down there. She was there for a whole minute and never heard it hit the ground. Stepping closer with her mind wandering, she kicked something heavy beneath her feet, knocking Roberto's bag down into the pit.

'Oh, shit,' she said, failing to reach it in time. After waiting around for a bit longer, the bag had vanished into the darkness, too, along with the water bottle. 'Eh, she doesn't need it. But I'll be back for you,' she said, addressing the sewer directly as she picked at her chin. 'Whatever you are.'

As she climbed out of the storm drain, satisfied at a job – not well done, but at least attempted with some degree of success – her bottle of water soon made an impact, exploding, and provoking a loud screech from the crab it landed on.

The other crabs around it noticed, too, and as they looked upwards towards the light, clicking their claws and running their tiny fingers across their mandibles, a bag slapped against the concrete, and they began to ascend from the pit in a number that would've been impossible to count in the dark. They couldn't come out, not yet. It was too bright, too obvious, so they were just waiting for the right time; for the night to come.

And the night was always coming.

CHAPTER TWELVE

AN ACTUAL, SOLVED MYSTERY

Naomi had been hooked up to life support the second they got her through the door.

Maddie had a hard time convincing the nurses that she, too, didn't need medical attention, due to all the blood she was covered in. She told them she was fine, and Anna told them it wasn't her blood anyway, which didn't help either, especially when they saw her missing finger that, a day before, hadn't been missing.

Sat alone on the waiting room chairs tapping her feet, Anna flicked through her phone now that she'd finally gotten some reception back, finding two new emails in her inbox, both labelled with the same subject line.

Help Me.

Maddie, on the other hand, stood by Naomi's bedside with Roberto. She'd only noticed it once they brought her into the light, but Naomi's appearance still unsettled Maddie a great deal. She was pale, yes, which was to be expected after having your hand cut off and slowly bleeding to death for god knows how long, but there was more to her than that. Her skin was loose and slimy when they first brought her in, and just like with Jon – the man who collapsed at Anna's front door a day previous – she was covered in thick, pus-filled boils.

Something had attacked Naomi, and that same something had attacked Jon; Maddie knew this now. So, why were they still both alive?

'We'll be out there if you need us,' said Maddie, patting Roberto on the shoulder. 'Just give us a shout.'

'Thanks,' he replied. 'Really. You said you'd be able to help and... I'm thankful that you did.'

'Don't thank us, yet,' said Maddie. 'Anna is almost certainly expecting a hefty payment for all the nothing she did.'

Roberto smiled. 'I'm sure she is.'

Back in the waiting room, which was riddled with mostly empty chairs and had a blank whiteboard clamped to the wall, Maddie sidled up to Anna and thought of resting her head against hers, just to relax for a moment, before deciding against it.

You're not together, she reminded herself. *She wouldn't want that, don't be stupid. You'll just distract her.*

'What are you looking for?' Maddie asked.

Anna tossed her phone over to Maddie and pointed at the screen. 'Does that make any sense to you?' she asked. 'Looks like bollocks to me. I can't make heads or tails of it.'

It was an email, the first of the two.

'I think someone needs help,' said Maddie.

'How'd you figure that?'

'Because the subject line is "help me," the first line says "help me," six times in a row, and on the by-line...'

'It says "help me"?' Anna interrupted.

'No, actually. It's just three letters. F.A.P.'

'Fap?' said Anna, jolting back in her chair. 'What the fuck?'

'No, you idiot. It's an acronym.'

'Oh, well, what does it mean?'

'It doesn't say.'

'Google it.'

'I'm not Googling the word fap.'

'Alright, fine,' she said, snapping her fingers. 'What else can you get from the email?'

'Whoever it is, they're lost. They say that they don't know where they are.'

'Well, that's bloody helpful. It's probably just a fake; somebody tryin' to spook me.'

'Probably,' said Maddie, handing the phone back. 'Creepy, though.'

'Sure is.' Anna quickly slipped the phone back into her coat pocket.

The two sat together awkwardly for a moment.

'So,' said Maddie. 'What are you thinking?'

'You stink,' Anna replied, quickly. 'Like, really bad.'

Maddie looked down at her plaid flannel which had since been covered in a dark, greenish liquid. 'I haven't had a chance to shower,' she said. 'I've been a bit preoccupied.'

'Well, you two can head home,' she said, jumping up. 'I got stuff to do.'

Maddie shrugged. 'What stuff? You actually solved a mystery for once. Have the evening off.'

'But aliens exist,' said Anna. 'I can't take the evening off when aliens exist.'

'What does that even mean, Anna? It could just be one alien, and they might not even be aliens. They seem more like, I don't know, monsters. What if it was just some kind of escaped experiment?'

'That's unlikely.'

'More likely than aliens.'

Anna puffed out her cheeks. She wasn't happy about considering a world when her so-called alien was just a regular crab but bigger and with more dangly bits.

That wasn't fun. There was no mystery to that.

Maddie stood up and placed one of her hands on Anna's shoulder. 'Are you okay?' she asked, after looking into her eyes and seeing how bloodshot they were.

'I'm fine,' Anna replied, fast. 'I'm fine. Don't worry.'

'You didn't get much sleep again, did you?'

Anna's eyes darted all around the room. The last words she'd heard from the Outsider were still stuck in her head.

Until next time, Annie. Closer than you think.

'Just a bad dream,' she mumbled, eventually. 'That's all.'

'What happens in it?'

Anna met her gaze. 'Does it matter?'

Maddie took one of Anna's hands with her own and lightly ran her fingers across her palm. 'I'm just worried about you.'

'Don't be,' said Anna, pulling away. 'I'm fine.'

Maddie nodded, although she didn't believe her. 'Okay.'

She turned back to the room that Roberto was still standing in, and the two locked eyes for a moment. She saw the look on his face. He was happy, somewhere under there, but on the surface, he looked almost lifeless. There was little hope in his eyes, before they sunk into his hands again, out of sight.

'He's going to need friends,' said Maddie, turning to Anna. 'What do you say? He can hang out with us tonight, right?'

'What?' Anna replied. 'I already told you, I'm not going out. It's not my thing.'

'Then we'll have a night in, at yours. Sound good?'

'No.'

'Well, that's too bad,' said Maddie, smiling. 'You've got to work on the sympathy part of your job, otherwise, you'll never be a good detective.'

'That's all secondary,' Anna scoffed, picking at the hairs on her neck. 'I can detect stuff. That's all I need.'

'Oh yeah? What about the money?'

'Oh fuck!' said Anna, scaring an old lady that wobbled past her down the corridor. 'Oh fuck.' She whispered that time. 'Six days. Six days until Steve throws me out.'

'Stanley.'

'Whatever. Shit.'

'Well then,' said Maddie, throwing one of her arms around Anna's shoulder, staring off into Naomi's emergency room where Roberto – Anna's last hope – was waiting. 'How about that night in?'

CHAPTER THIRTEEN

HELP ME

It'd been almost a day since Geoff Tilbrook's house collapsed around him and the Outsider pulled him from the edge of death. He was hungry, lost, lonely, and very, very confused.

He had walked up and down this strange new place he'd been dropped into countless times, failing to find an exit, or much at all, really. He started to think that, just maybe, this is what death really felt like. It was dark and seemingly infinite, yet, still made him feel trapped. The walls would move all around him, and sometimes the ground would shake, throwing him all over the place.

It was always a soft landing. The ground was light and damp, as were the walls and, if he could've found a way to reach the ceiling above him, he'd have realised that the whole cave was like that.

Yes, Geoff thought, wandering aimlessly. *It's a cave. But a cave made of what? Flesh? That's not a real thing.*

Occasionally, Geoff would come across a series of green, fluorescent lights, drooping down from the ceiling like a pair of pendulous testicles; helping him find his way. He spent the night under one of them. At least, he assumed it was the night. There was no real way to tell, as the cave of flesh didn't exactly have any windows.

He pushed on, into a cavern so large that it made his cottage look tiny in comparison. He knew this because his cottage was *inside* the cavern. A bit more rubble-y than he was used to, yes, but it was unmistakable, as the sign on his front door – the number seven – had been embedded in the ground.

Reaching down, he pulled the sign out with a pop and watched as the wound in the cave repaired itself. He looked up, stumbled backwards as his brain thumped in his skull, and passed out on the floor.

A dream came to him.

It was fast and confusing; his brain trying to process the last twenty-four hours into something that made actual sense. He was in his house again. It was shaking. He looked down, paintings falling off the walls, baked beans covering the floor, before the whole damn place collapsed under his feet and the thing below widened its jaws, swallowing him and his house in one, quick gulp.

He woke up, dazed, and started to panic. He was inside that creature. He had to be.

This will help you get out of the worm, the Outsider's voice echoed. *Don't let me down.*

'Oh, no,' said Geoff, bolting upright and slamming his head on a chunk of debris, nearly knocking himself out as he fumbled his phone from his pocket and into his hands.

He pulled out the card from earlier, squinted at the details, and hammered out an email to the first address on there. His head was killing him and the light from the screen had blurred into one big blob, so, he just typed the first thing he thought of.

Help me. That was the subject line. He tapped the body of the email and kept on typing.

Help me. Help me. Help me. Help me. Help me. Help me.

Next line.

I don't know where I am. I don't understand. Please help me.

Next line. He didn't know what to type. What had the stranger said again? Those three words, what were they?

F.A.P. he wrote, eventually, quickly sending the email as the fear of the dwindling battery sped him up.

You need more detail, he thought, and before he faded into the darkness again, he typed out another email.

Subject line.

Help me.

Next line.

Giant worm. GIANT WORM. NEED HELP. HELP ME.

It was on the tip of his tongue, but he couldn't quite get it, so he signed it off the same way as before. Three letters.

F.A.P.

He hit send, buried his face in the flesh under him, and slept in the dark.

CHAPTER FOURTEEN

THREE CARD SHUFFLE

Having finished putting together a makeshift sofa out of Anna's spare mattress, pillows and assortment of other random crap, Maddie offered Roberto a seat, took his coat, and asked everyone if they wanted a coffee.

'Tea, please,' said Roberto, undoing his tie. 'Thank you.'

That's not a coffee, thought Anna. *Cheeky bastard.*

It was entirely possible she said it, too, as Maddie was giving her one hell of a death stare. 'And for you?' she asked.

'Coffee, ta,' said Anna.

'Nine sugars?'

'Ten. Cheers.'

Maddie had given up questioning it anymore and got to boiling the kettle instead. Something caught her eye, though, floating in a jar.

Anna's ring finger.

'Ugh, gross,' said Maddie.

''Ello, ya little bastard,' Anna said, sliding over to her finger-jar and flicking it. 'You alright in there?'

It was looking greener and fatter than before, with plump boils having popped the fingernail off; letting it float around in the vinegar.

'You really need to get rid of that thing,' said Maddie.

'You really need to have a shower,' Anna replied. 'Smelly sod.'

'I will. And you know what you're going to do, don't you?' She nodded towards Roberto, sitting on a pale cushion.

'Oh, yeah,' said Anna. 'I was hoping you could do the whole nice part. Make him like us, y'know?'

'Absolutely not,' Maddie replied. 'That's down to you. You didn't want my help earlier, remember?'

'Well, yeah, but this is different,' she whispered. 'I can't talk to that bastard. What would I say?'

'Just be nice. Be sympathetic, and, who knows. You might end up enjoying talking to people.'

Anna retched. 'People slow me down. Don't want it. Don't need it.'

'You *do* need it. You can start by not referring to him as "that bastard" when he's sitting right behind you, and very much in earshot.'

Oh shit.

'Right, there's your coffee,' said Maddie, tossing the spoon into the sink. 'I'm going for a shower. Do you have spare clothes I can borrow?'

'Sure. In my wardrobe, bottom drawer.'

'Are they going to fit me?'

Anna didn't reply to that.

'Okay,' Maddie went on, sliding a mug of tea across the worktop. 'Take this to him, and be nice.'

'I'm always nice.'

'You're literally never nice.'

'Fuck off.'

Maddie smirked and left for the bathroom. Coming into Anna's room first, though, she went straight for the wardrobe, finding some spare clothes neatly folded at the bottom that were not only suited to her style but were also, surprisingly, exactly in her size.

Odd, she thought, seeing as how she was a full foot taller than Anna and then some. Anna would've gone out of her way to buy them, and for what reason?

Maddie pushed that thought aside and went for a shower.

'So,' said Anna, carrying Roberto's tea over to him, spilling a good quarter of it along the way with her constant shakes and jitters. 'How's it going?'

Good, she thought. *That was good.*

'Better, thank you,' said Roberto; his voice was sweet, really. 'Would you like to sit—'

'No,' said Anna, suddenly. 'I mean, no, thank you. I am good standing.'

Her voice was so static it was like she'd been replaced by a robot in the last ten to fifteen minutes, and now that Roberto had seen giant, heavily armoured crab-monsters he almost considered that a genuine possibility.

Stranger things had happened, after all.

Roberto shuffled in his seated position, looking around his feet. 'Have you seen my bag?' he asked, having seemingly forgotten about it since finding Naomi.

'Oh,' said Anna. 'Yeah, I kicked it off a ledge.'

'Oh.'

'Yeah. My bad.'

Idiot.

'It wasn't on purpose, though.'

Roberto sighed, but understood all the same.

'Madeleine was telling me that you've been having some money problems,' he asked, sensing her distress. 'How much do I owe you?'

Thank Christ, she thought. *That got me out of jail.*

'Oh, good question,' said Anna, dashing over to the kitchen cupboard, the one with the hole in it, and fumbling around for her rent contract. 'Seven hundred and eighty-four pounds.'

Roberto's eyes nearly fell out.

'And thirty-two pence.'

'That's... That's quite a lot,' said Roberto.

'That's the cost of progress, my friend,' she said back. 'You got it?'

'Well, not exactly.'

'Goddammit. Well, I can't exactly take your wife back, now, can I?'

What was that? Anna thought to herself, almost as if Maddie were critiquing her from inside her own head. *Was that supposed to be fucking funny?*

'I can pay you something, though,' said Roberto, standing up. 'Will five-hundred be enough?'

'What? No, of course it won't, dude, I need—'

She paused, seeing the look on the man's face, forcing a smile as he tried his best to be reasonable. She needed the money, all of it, and she knew that, but she'd also never been paid so much for solving a crime before. This was a big deal.

'Fuck,' she said to herself, forcing a smile in return. 'That'll be fine.'

'Do I write you a cheque, or...?'

'PayPal!' she blurted out. 'I mean... PayPal would be best,' she went on, making her voice sound more innocent and gentle. 'Thank you.'

Roberto noticed and then paid her anyway. His wife was back, and alive. Critical, but alive, which was all he cared about.

Anna took out her phone, her face lighting up when the payment came through, even if she were still two-hundred quid short. Back to her emails, now ignoring the man she'd gotten her money from, she decided to check the other one that she didn't get around to.

Just like the first, it was marked *"Help me"*.

She danced around the room as she read it aloud, holding it close to her face, inverting the colours, holding it further away from her face, zooming in, zooming out; anything she could think of to discover the email's secrets.

Conclusion; it was just an email.

'Giant worm,' she said, casually, as if it weren't that strange of a sentence. 'Giant worm. Need help. Help me.' She squinted at the end. 'Fap?'

Roberto spat out his tea. 'I'm sorry?'

'Nothing,' Anna replied. 'Just another case.'

'Oh, right,' Roberto nodded. 'You get a lot of those?'

'Uh-huh.' She didn't even look at him. She was too busy rubbing her eyeballs and flicking her cheeks. 'Giant worm. Giant worm. Giant... Worm...'

'So, how long have you been doing this?' Roberto asked.

'What?' Anna replied, looking from the screen to Roberto and back again. 'I dunno. Couple months. Maybe more.'

'And you've made a living this way?'

Anna paused for a second and shrugged. 'Yeah, I guess so.'

'Right.' Roberto leaned forward from his seated position, hands resting on his black business trousers. 'What did you do before this?'

'Well, I...' Her eyes went blank. 'Not much, I suppose.'

'Where's your family?'

'Excuse me?'

The tone with which she bit back at him caused him to retreat himself into the cushions. 'You're just very young, is all,' he said. 'I didn't move out of my folks' until I was almost thirty.'

Anna swallowed and her throat clicked. 'That's nice,' she said. 'I dunno. I don't know where they are, and I don't think about it.'

'I'm sure you could...'

'I'm not talking about this,' Anna blurted out, suddenly, for once giving him her full attention. 'I don't even know you, man.'

Roberto jolted suddenly, feeling sheepish. 'Okay,' he said. 'Sorry.'

Anna started pacing around the room, again, her concentration more scattered than usual.

Maddie burst in a few moments later, all cleaned up. 'What's this?' she asked, drying her hair before sitting herself next to Roberto, who shuffled himself into his own corner. 'Another client?'

'Maybe,' Anna replied, fumbling her words. 'Gimme a sec.'

She dashed out of the room and leapt onto her bare bed, slamming her bedroom door behind her before firing an email back at the sender, leaving her name and phone number.

Contact me, ASAP, it read. *I can help you. P.S. Have money.*

That wasn't all she did, though, and once she set her phone down on the bedside chest of drawers, she pulled the bottom one out and searched through it. It didn't take long to find what she was looking for. Scraps of old receipts from years ago – when she bought a *Snickers* bar from a place she'd forgotten about in a town she never visited and had no desire to – made up most of the contents. She pulled them out, placed them on the bed, and then reached in for a small, black, wallet-like container. She opened it, pulling back the rubber strap that kept both sides of it together, and looked inside.

There were three cards in it, all of them an aged, yellowish colour with the text on them still intact. She only pulled out one. It had a number on it; a landline. She bit into her lip hard and hammered the number into her phone, hovering her finger over the call button. Her hands were shaking. She was going to ring them, whoever they were. It was easy. It was just one button away.

She backspaced it, and tossed the wallet back into the drawer, having thrown the receipts in just beforehand so that it was resting on top of them.

Idiot, she thought to herself, hearing Roberto's questions echoing in her head. *You never thought about it before. Don't think about it now.*

She laid down flat on her bed, her legs dangling off the edge as she pinched her eyes together, knowing that, even though she hadn't called anybody, she'd gotten ever so slightly closer to doing so.

She'd saved the number in her phone before deleting it, under a single, uncertain word, and that word had made itself known in her head for the first time in three years.

Home?

***

Meanwhile, Maddie and Roberto got chatting in the living room.

'So, what do you think?' she asked. 'Anna. How is she?'

Roberto took a deep breath. 'She's intense.'

'Yeah.'

'She's weird.'

'That too.'

'She's a bit crazy.'

'Oh yeah. That's the main three, to be honest.'

Roberto grinned. 'Why does she keep doing that?' he asked.

'Doing what?'

'She's always flailing around the place, snapping her fingers. Does she even sit down, ever?'

'Not really,' Maddie replied. 'She's always been like that. She has a lot of energy and can't always concentrate.'

'And she's a detective?'

'Wants to be, yeah.'

Roberto squinted. 'Interesting combination. I always thought you needed good concentration for a job like that.'

'Yeah,' she said. 'Me too.'

There was a long pause between the two of them, and Maddie was staring at the floor like it was home to the most interesting carpet ever created.

'I think you should tell her how you feel,' Roberto said, suddenly. 'It'd be good for you.'

'What, now?' Maddie replied. 'What do you mean?'

He shot her a glare.

'Oh, no, god. It's not like that. We've just known each other for a long time, and, we're very good friends.'

'Sure you are,' said Roberto, winking. 'Only the very best of friends ogle each other all day long. I see why you let her walk in-front.'

'Oh, Jesus.' She paused, running one of her hands through her hair as she gave herself a moment, trying to hide her smile. 'What can I say? She does look very nice from the back.'

'Knew it,' said Roberto. 'Tell her, you idiot. I'm serious.'

'No. It's stupid. You've met her. She doesn't have time for anything or anyone. She's a... malfunctioning robot. I can't sit down and have the talk with her because she never bloody sits down. I'd have to pin her down to get something out of her.'

'Well, you said it.' Maddie didn't have time to clock that one before Roberto had already moved on. 'She must have a sensitive side.'

'I've never seen it.'

'Then, what else do you see in her, if not that?'

The question stopped Maddie stone dead, and she thought on it for a while, her eyes noticeably rolling around her head as she tried to find the words. She had answers, lots of them. She wanted to say everything, but that wasn't *really* an answer, not for someone as curious as Roberto.

He was looking for specifics.

'Most people are so boring,' said Maddie, finally, cracking her knuckles. 'I mean, you saw the excitement on her face earlier.'

'Well, it was quite dark in that sewer,' said Roberto, 'so, not really.'

Maddie frowned but carried on. 'I don't think I've ever seen someone be as passionate about anything as she is about this. She cares, even if it's rarely about me.'

Roberto lifted one leg and placed it over the other, taking a sip of his tea. 'I think you're both weird as hell. I look forward to seeing how it goes.'

Maddie turned to Roberto. 'You've lightened up, all of a sudden.'

'What can I say?' he replied. 'I'm always curious.'

'Seems that way.'

'Listen, I think you should let her know,' he said, setting down his mug. 'I might not get the chance to tell Nay what I really think about her ever again, and I hate it.'

'You don't know that.'

'Do you want to know what the last thing I ever said to her was? I called her an arsehole. It was a joke, and she knew that but...'

'It's not the last thing you'd want her to hear.'

'Yeah,' said Roberto, standing up. 'Think about it.'

'Are you leaving?'

'Yes. I'm tired, and I thought it'd be best to leave you two alone for a while.'

'Right,' Maddie nodded. 'Okay, well, have a safe journey home.'

'Thanks,' Roberto replied. 'I would say the same to you, but, you're probably going to end up staying the night.'

'Oh, sod off.'

He shut the door, locking it behind him, leaving Maddie on her own for a few minutes until the toilet flushed and Anna came bumbling into the living room.

'Roger's gone, then,' said Anna, eyes glued to her laptop.

Maddie stared vacantly off into the distance for a second before her eyes locked onto Anna and she looked her up and down; over and over.

Goddammit, Roberto, she thought. *You bastard.*

Maddie stood up. 'Hey,' she said. 'Everything alright?'

'Peachy,' Anna replied, looking up from her laptop for just a moment. 'Why?'

'I... I was wondering if we could talk about something. I'll be quick.'

Anna wasn't really paying attention, as her eyes drifted back down towards her empty Twitter, but still, she nodded.

'Sure, whatever,' she said. 'What do ya wanna talk about?'

CHAPTER FIFTEEN

CODE BLUE

Roberto didn't go home right away. Instead, he spent some time, not much, by Naomi's bedside whenever he could, in-between the nurses coming in and wiping away all the built-up goo from her skin.

One of the nurses remembered him. Her name was Andria. She said he was looking well. He said nothing at all.

Out in the hallways people were chatting amongst themselves; frightened people, and Roberto, being Roberto, eavesdropped on nearly all of it. More sinkhole talk came up, a lot more. Small ones, medium ones, absolutely bloody massive ones; it didn't matter. They'd been more frequent, as if the whole of South Marshwood was going to collapse at any moment, and perhaps it was.

Roberto didn't care about that. He'd move, and Naomi would come with him.

He looked at her, lying in that hospital bed, looking as if she'd caught the plague, and felt like shit all over again.

You should've tried harder, he thought, thinking about how she was yanked away from him. *You could've stopped it.* He tried not to think like that, but when there wasn't much else to think about, what choice did he have?

Another twenty minutes went by. He didn't move a muscle, except when one of the nurses told him to, before they heard an alarm beep from down the hallway and they rushed out of the emergency room.

It was a code blue. Roberto knew that because, well, the announcement said that it was, and Roberto had ears, but he also knew what a code blue was. An emergency, probably a heart attack, but almost definitely something bad. He tried to ignore it. It wasn't his place to interfere. It was nothing to do with him. His place was with his wife.

He peered through the window. Surveying the situation didn't mean he was involved, absolutely not. And when he left Naomi's bedside, told her he'd be right back – leaving the door ajar to follow the rush of hospital staff – that was just to satisfy his curiosity. He was *not* getting involved.

'What's happening?' he asked one of the nurses. 'Is everything okay?'

Goddammit.

The bright lights were on in another of the emergency rooms as one man – in a state not too dissimilar to Naomi's – thrashed about on the bed. His skin had become thick and blobby, expanding outwards as if he were a water balloon, slowly filling up.

Ready to burst.

Two doctors and an equal number of nurses rushed in to try and settle him down. One had a needle full of anaesthetic at the ready, but when they tried to find somewhere to plunge it, they couldn't find a spot that wouldn't immediately burst open when pricked. If the seizure wasn't going to kill the poor bastard, then that infection surely would.

Roberto wanted a closer look. He wanted to hear what was happening, so he snuck through the first set of double doors, peering over the window in the second with it barely hanging open.

Good job, not getting involved, Roberto thought. *Arsehole.*

'Mister Peterson,' Roberto heard one of the doctors say, fully dressed in blue and sporting a pale beard snood. 'I'm going to need you to calm down, okay? Talk to me. What's happening?'

Jon Peterson, the patient, stopped dead still for a moment. His eyes snapped towards the doctor and he reached out for him, grabbing him by the apron.

'W-W-Where is she?' he yelled. 'She was supposed to be here!'

'There's no-one here but us, sir,' the doctor replied. 'You're perfectly safe, we just need you to settle down so that we can sort things out.'

'I need to find her. He said he'd only let me live if I found her.'

'You're safe,' the doctor repeated. 'No man is coming here to hurt you. You are perfectly safe with us.'

'You don't understand,' said Jon, his voice shaking. 'I was going to die. I would've died and he saved me and if I don't get him what he wants...'

'We sedating him?' interrupted one of the nurses, her needle at the ready. 'Talking to him isn't helping. Look at his heart rate.'

It'd broken two-hundred and was still climbing.

'Jesus Christ,' said the other doctor. 'Where are you gonna stick him? He looks like Mister Blobby, but, y'know, green.'

'What are you saying?'

'I'm saying you might burst him.'

The doctor looked at his patient. 'We might just have to.'

The four of them looked around at each other until, at last, they nodded.

'Hold him down. If you find a chance to get that needle into him then you take it, clear?'

The nurse nodded, and the other three people in the room who weren't covered in blobs held Jon to the bed, being careful of his extra blubber and to not tear it more than they had to. Jon started to scream again. He shouldn't have been able to make a noise that high.

That sounds familiar, thought Roberto. *I've heard that before.*

The doctor's grasp slipped and Jon launched himself out of the hospital bed and onto the ground, splattering some of his pustules across the floor and up one of the nurse's legs. Everyone stood away from him, and as his head snapped backwards, he stared directly into Roberto's eyes through the glass window.

There was silence all around until, at last, Jon spoke his final three words. Three words that a stranger had told him in the darkness, just after his life was about to end for the first time; a promise that he needed to keep.

'Find. Anna. Pendleton.'

CHAPTER SIXTEEN

FINGERED

Anna's severed finger, floating in the jar, started to move. The boils had inflated until the whole thing had become one big, gross super-boil. But she hadn't noticed, not yet.

'Well?' Anna asked, staring at Maddie. 'What is it?'

Maddie's feet shuffled involuntarily. She hadn't thought this through. She didn't know what she was going to say. They'd known each other for ages, why was this so hard? Steadying herself, eventually, Maddie held her hands together and spoke.

'I—'

'Hold on, me first,' said Anna, barging in.

Was she waiting just to do that?

'A new sinkhole opened up a few miles away,' she went on, sticking her laptop on the floor. 'Big fucker. Swallowed some poor bastard's house by the sounds of it. I was thinking of heading down and checking it out. You comin'?'

'You're asking me?' Maddie replied. 'I thought you didn't want help with this.'

'Well, yeah, but it went alright last time, eh?'

'Are you sure we should be going? It'll be dark in a couple of hours.'

'Oh, c'mon, someone might need our help,' she said.

Huh, Maddie thought. *That's nice of—*

'And they might have money!'

Never mind.

'Anyway, I'm gonna head down there now. Who knows? Might be able to stop these things. You're welcome to tag along.'

'Y-You think there's more?'

'Definitely. There's no way there's just one of those crabby bastards.'

'We're still not calling them that,' Maddie whispered.

Anna was serious. She placed her hand on the doorknob and went to yank it open, before she was stopped by Maddie wrapping her hand around Anna's from behind and pushing the door closed again.

'Stay,' she whispered, close to her ear. 'Stay with me.'

Anna shivered. 'Erm... No, if that's cool. You can stay if you want, but I'm offski.'

Holding Anna by the waist, Maddie spun her around and gently pushed her against the door. 'You're tired,' she said. 'So am I. I was thinking of going to bed. *You're* welcome to tag along if you want.'

Anna's eyes widened, with a smile. 'What?' she said. 'What are you—'

There was a crash. The jar with Anna's mutated, severed finger hit the apartment floor, spraying vinegar and broken glass across the carpet.

'What the fuck?' asked Anna, hitting her head on the door before barging Maddie out of the way, looking for the source of the noise. 'What was that?' A pause. 'Oh, shit.'

Maddie sighed, eyes on her feet, slowly pivoting towards her. 'What is it?'

'It's missing.' Anna was on her knees. Her nostrils flared up. She gagged. 'It's fucking missing.'

'What's missing?'

'My finger. Oh, fuck. Fuck, fuck, fuck.'

She danced around the apartment. She couldn't see it anywhere. Not because it was particularly hard to find, but because she was a bit of an idiot.

'There,' Maddie pointed.

The two of them locked eyes with the green, pulsating blob on the floor, as it slowly rolled its way towards them.

'That doesn't look right,' said Anna. 'My finger wasn't *that* weird.'

The blob stopped in full view of both of them. They figured it to be the size of a small mouse, which was strange, but then they noticed it was alive, which was even stranger. A large split then formed down the centre of the blob, from front to back.

Neither of them knew what to do. Maddie had gone from tired to horny to very, very confused, and Anna had just skipped straight to the last one.

'I'm gonna poke it,' said Anna.

'You're not going to poke it,' Maddie replied. 'I forbid it.'

'Bite me.'

Creeping closer to the blob, Anna peered inwards, ready to give it a quick jab with her finger, when it tore itself open. The outer layer peeled off, spilling more gross shit into the carpet until there was only one thing left in its place.

A small, crab-like monster.

'Oh my god,' said Anna, eyebrows raised. 'It's adorable!'

The crab screeched in her face, and before she knew where she was, Maddie had thrown her to the floor and kicked it across the room.

It hurt like hell.

'Ow, bastard!' she yelled, holding her foot.

The crab hit the wall and was wedged into it, quickly flipping itself over to scale upwards, sticking itself to and crawling over the ceiling towards them.

'Oh, shit. What's it doing now?' Anna asked.

'How the hell should I know?'

The baby crab was getting ready to drop, and so, as it began to detach itself from the ceiling, Maddie reached for Anna's laptop, slamming the lid shut and holding it like a bat.

'Hey!' said Anna. 'Don't use that. That was expensive.'

'Yeah, yeah,' Maddie replied. 'Whatever.'

She swung the laptop like she was playing baseball, cheering as she belted the crab out of the air. The casing of the laptop cracked right down the centre and the crab bounced across the apartment floor, coming to a stop towards the back wall where it staggered about for a few seconds.

'Come 'ere, fucko!' Anna yelled.

She stomped on the crab with her boot, crushing it underfoot into a green thick and crunchy paste. She wiped her shoe off on the ground and kicked them both off her feet, dashing back over to Maddie with a delighted look on her face.

Anna and Maddie locked eyes as they, out of breath, smiled at one another; a result of their small, but exciting victory.

'This is huge,' said Anna. 'We just witnessed the birth of a crab butt-tooth alien first-hand!' She was bouncing on the spot, squeezing Maddie's shoulders. 'You know what we gotta do now, right?'

'Absolutely,' she replied.

She had Anna pinned to the ground before she even knew what was happening, clutching her wrists tight as their lips fought each other.

'Whoa,' said Anna, catching some air as her pupils stretched. 'What are you doing?'

'What does it look like?' Maddie growled before she ran her hands down to Anna's waist and slipped her tongue in her mouth.

Anna shut her eyes tight, holding Maddie closely, before they snapped back open. 'This isn't the time,' she said, pulling away again. 'We need to...'

'You need to shut up,' Maddie whispered, biting her lip. 'Okay?'

Anna didn't know what to do, or if she should do anything. The way Maddie was speaking, it reminded her of how she had been in the sewer earlier that day, cutting a crab-monster to pieces; or, for that matter, about ten seconds ago, when she cracked a baby one in the face with Anna's very expensive and now-totally-broken laptop.

It was real. It was passionate. It was scary.

She was really into it.

'You're not shaking,' said Maddie, her head slightly raised. 'You're actually still.'

Anna had never been still before in her life; even when sleeping she'd be all over the place, but in that moment, she was calm. She was content.

Then her phone rang. She jimmied it out of her pocket, and before she had the chance to even see the number, Maddie took it from her and tossed it across the room.

'Hey, that might be important.'

'As important as this?'

A beat.

'God, no,' Anna replied, resting her cold, not-fully-fingered hand on Maddie's cheek. 'I... have questions. Lots of questions. I—' Warm breath hit Anna's neck and made her shiver. 'Oh, fuck. They can wait, though.'

'Thought so.'

Anna pulled Maddie in and kissed her deeply. She wasn't great at it, but that didn't matter. 'Wanna take this into my room?'

'No,' Maddie whispered, sliding her fingers into the top of Anna's jeans. 'I want you, right here.'

There was a pause. Her usual retort would be to argue with that and go on about how the bed was comfier and more practical and warmer and better in basically every way, but she didn't.

She didn't say anything, except for what Maddie wanted to hear.

CHAPTER SEVENTEEN

AND THEN THEY HAD SEX

'I love you,' said Maddie.

Anna met her gaze, and, at last, she said it back.

'I love you, too.'

CHAPTER EIGHTEEN

POP ART

Jon exploded in the middle of the emergency room, splatter-ing the windows, walls, and everyone inside it with a thick green fluid. The impact made most people jump, turn away, and run like hell. Roberto, however, had a different reaction, even after Jon's plump intestine slapped against the window right in front of his face.

Screaming came from either side of him. A man just ex-ploded, after all, but then the screams kept going, only to be gradually silenced by either distance or something much worse.

Don't get involved. Don't get involved.

Roberto peered through the door. The mess that was Jon's corpse only began to spread, as out from his now-deflated body poured tens – if not hundreds – of baby crab-monsters. The floor was soon covered in them, like a swarm of locusts, as they all converged on the piece of meat closest to them.

The nurse with the needle.

She stamped a few of them into a chunky paste, but a doz-en or two more managed to scuttle up her trouser leg, where they slashed her flesh open and crawled their way inside. She started thrashing about, with little bumps appearing all over her skin, moving around as the crabs burrowed their way through her flesh. She opened her mouth to scream. Some crabs crawled out of her mouth from the inside. Some crabs crawled into her mouth from the outside, and then she hit the ground; dead.

Roberto jolted backwards, only then noticing the other three people still in the room. Two had since been overwhelmed, pinned to the floor and torn to pieces by sharp snapping claws and spindly fingers. There was one man left, the doctor, who tripped over on his way to the door. He scampered backwards, struggling to find a grip, all as the sea of crabs swept towards him.

Don't get involved, Roberto thought. *This is not your place. Run. Now.*

He yanked the door open into the emergency room, threw his arms around the doctor's shoulders and hoisted his arse out of there, laying him upright against the wall to catch his breath for a moment.

'You're okay,' said Roberto. 'You made it.'

And then he got a closer look, seeing that two crabs had clung to the doctor's face and were sucking his eyeballs out. There was a pop as they retracted their teeth and fell from the poor man's face, landing in his lap with the teeth on their underbelly glistening in the light.

'Oh,' Roberto said, staggering backwards. 'Shit.'

He turned on his heels and ran the other way, not looking back as the ground behind him was covered in more of those things, the lights above the corridor bouncing bright rays all over the hospital. They scuttled towards him, and just him, as he was coming up to the room that his wife was still bedridden in.

You left the door ajar, he remembered. *You idiot. You arsehole.*

He wanted to keep running. It would've made sense to keep running, but he couldn't, not without making sure she was going to be – if not safe – at least safer. He thought about locking himself in with her, waiting it out, but who would get help then? The public?

Not bloody likely.

He swung a hard left and ran towards her emergency room, found the door, and yanked it hard until it was firmly jammed in the doorframe. There was only a slight gap at the bottom, but as the swarm of crabs pursued him further, he prayed that they were just a bit too big to fit through it.

They had him mostly surrounded, hopping up at him to try and catch hold of his clothes and skin as he ran back past them. A few of them managed to snag his jacket, sinking their mandibles into his clothes. He quickly threw himself against the wall on his way past to shake them, splattering green gunk across it in a big smear. He could see the door. It was close, and with the sun still peering above the trees in a warm orange glow, it felt like freedom.

It was freedom. He didn't know what he was going to do once he got out there, as a quick glance over his shoulder informed him that, yes, they were still absolutely fucking everywhere. He tried not to think about it.

The doors slid open and Roberto rushed outside, bumbling his way down the stairs and getting caught on the bottom one, landing on his front and skidding across the concrete on his face. That nose wasn't going to heal anytime soon.

Well done, he thought. *You've been defeated by stairs, Roberto. Bloody stairs.*

He rolled over, saw the swarm of crabs scuttling towards him, and braced himself. With his eyes closed, he only heard it happen. The sound of crackling firewood, or broken bones, over and over again. He opened his eyes and saw the crabs as they popped right in front of him, like firecrackers, splattering burnt monster blood all across the hospital stairs. Some of them aimlessly wandered around for a bit, alive but confused, until their faint armoured shells withered away, as did their bodies.

'What in the world?' he said to himself, hand around his nose to hold the blood in.

He stood up, limped a little, and turned around. It hit him there and then as the sun was hanging, somewhat proudly, in the sky.

Delighted, even, at a job well done.

CHAPTER NINETEEN

COME AGAIN

Anna slipped her jeans back on before anything else. It was harder than it looked. She'd never had to sneak away from a sleeping, peaceful, and barely dressed Maddie before, or anyone for that matter. She wasn't sure if it was something she'd get used to.

She wouldn't mind getting used to it, though; that was for sure.

She looked around the apartment for the rest of her stuff, which Maddie had tossed all over the place in her rush to stop Anna from wearing them. It was cute at the time, but now it was just a pain in the arse. Fully dressed, she grabbed her phone, saw six missed calls, swore under her breath, found her boots, and put them on. The right one was still a bit sticky on the bottom, and as she looked at the smashed corpse of the baby crab that'd caused it, she got onto her knees and gave it a quick lick.

'Ugh, gross,' she said, expecting nothing less. 'Metal, again.'

She gave it more of a look over, taking in the details. It had the armoured shell that the bigger ones had, but after being crushed with a quick stamp of a boot, they weren't nearly as durable. Underdeveloped, even.

Not just a baby, thought Anna. *But a really shit baby.*

She tossed it in the bin.

With her large raincoat now zipped up to her neck and her rucksack on her back – the flashlight and meat cleaver firmly tucked away inside – Anna slipped out of the apartment door, leaving Maddie exactly where she was, before locking it behind her. She wasn't being as gentle as she thought she was, but with her phone already calling back the number that'd tried so many times to get into contact with her, she put it out of her mind.

It didn't ring for long before they answered.

'H-Hello?' came a voice, male. 'I need help. Can you help me?'

'Are you the guy?' said Anna, walking into the elevator. 'What do you need?'

'Help me,' they said. 'Help me. Help me. Help me. I need help.'

'Yeah, yeah, I fucking gathered that from all the emails. What do you need help with? Where are you?'

'I'm lost. This place... it's toxic. My skin is loose. I can feel it.'

'Oi,' she said. 'I'm not asking again. Where are you?' she asked, again.

'Inside the worm.'

'What worm?'

The elevator pinged. She'd reached the ground floor.

'The giant worm. The man told me it was a worm. He said you could help me get out.'

'Come again? Giant worm?' Anna said to herself, ignoring the rest of what the man had told her.

'I-I-I know it sounds crazy.'

'I dunno, mate,' Anna replied, meaning it. 'It makes sense. I'll find you. Whack your GPS on and send me your location. I'll get you outta there in no time. Easy peasy.'

'Please hurry,' said the man, barely getting the words out. 'Battery is low.'

'You'd better get to it, then,' she replied. 'Oh, and what's your name? I'm going to assume it's not fap, and if it is, you have my sympathies.'

'Geoffrey,' said the man. 'Tilbrook.'

Huh, Anna thought. *I swear that name rings a bell.* And that was really saying something.

'Well then, Geoffrey,' she said. 'Hold tight. I'm on my way.' She hung up, grinning to herself.

I think I was just nice to someone.

After making it out of her apartment building in the last light of the day, the alert of Geoff's location popped up on her phone. It took a moment to register, but once it did, she saw where he was.

He was all over the damn place, circling around and through South Marshwood like he was flying a fighter jet on acid. The icon jittered this way and that, did loop-de-loops and even managed a perfect figure of eight at one point. The lack of service underground didn't exactly make it easy to follow, either.

She wasn't going to catch it like that. She needed to wait for it to settle down, first, like it had done when she first encountered it. She just needed to wait.

'I can wait,' she said to herself, shuffling her feet. 'I can easily wait. I'm really good at waiting.'

***

'I'M FUCKING BORED!' she yelled, three minutes later, scaring the absolute shit out of two passers-by on their way into town.

That was one strange thing that she noticed. Most people had been leaving town that afternoon, not entering it, so what was going on? She thought about it for a moment, quickly got bored of that, too, before going back to just being her regular variety of bored.

She looked at her phone. Geoff's tracker had slowed down quite a bit in the meantime, circling the same area over and over again. It wasn't far from her, in fact, she could even feel a slight rumble beneath her feet whenever it went around the right bend. It was circling the sewage system, perhaps it was even weaving itself directly through it. She ran there right away, glancing at her phone every few seconds to make sure it hadn't strayed too far and barrelling right through the forest.

Along the way, aside from the sun setting behind the horizon, she saw little else as the night moved inwards.

Arriving at the south bridge, Anna took out her flashlight and skidded down the embankment to reach the storm drain. She climbed inside. It was a lot less hassle when it was just her and, once again, she tried to slide butt-first down the decline. It was a failure.

No sliding, just a damp pair of trousers and an untapped opportunity for fun.

Anna had reached the catwalk when she heard the worm beneath her feet, sliding and crashing about the place as the GPS went haywire.

She yelled. It echoed. The worm didn't reply.

She started tapping on the railing and stomping her feet, too. To the untrained eye, it would look like she didn't have a plan, but that was it, apparently; get the worms attention.

Once the worm's attention had been got... well, she hadn't thought that far ahead.

'Oi!' she yelled. 'Pay attention to me!'

She shone her flashlight down into the shaft below and saw the red, fat body of the worm as it wriggled around below. Only the smallest part of the worm was visible, but even that part was, as Maddie would've put it, disconcertingly big.

'Hey!' More echoes. No reply.

Anna looked all around her, lighting up the walls to see if any crabs were going to ambush her. There weren't any in sight, which was good, but the out-of-sight had still gone unaccounted for. She wasn't intending to stick around for long.

She looked ahead of herself again, flashlight only catching up to her eyes moments later when she saw the light bounce back into her face, as if someone was holding a mirror up in front of her to try and blind her. She squinted a little, let her eyes adjust, just to see another half a dozen of them staring back at her.

The eyes were massive, bigger than her and with a black slit straight down the middle. Up close, she could see the detail on the iris, all dark and stretched into strands. Her flashlight wandered again until the true size of the monster covered her whole view.

It was the worm. It was real. It had paid attention to her. Small, tentacle-like appendages flapped about across the worms' face, moistening up the teeth. It took a while, as there must've been thousands of them.

You had a real plan, right? Her brain asked her. *This is when you use your plan, right? Hello? Are you there?*

Anna was staring gormlessly at the giant worm, hoping for her body to kick in, but it didn't. She'd wanted aliens to exist so badly, real aliens, but not ones that were this big. It was too much for one person to process.

So, she stood there, until the worm's jaw split open in three places and it splattered her with its saliva. After that, it puffed out its fat, bulbous neck, and went for a bite.

CHAPTER TWENTY

SPOILED MEAT

Maddie was woken up by a knock at the door. She rolled over to see that Anna had already left. She wasn't surprised, exactly, but she was a tad disappointed.

'One second,' Maddie called out, gathering her clothes and chucking them on. Her hair was a puffy mess, but she left it as is, and opened the door.

It was Roberto. He looked terrified.

'How's it going?' Maddie asked.

He barged in.

'Fair enough.'

'I need your help,' he said, sweating. 'I...' His eyes rolled around his skull for a bit. 'Does it smell weird in here?'

Maddie's face filled with blood. 'Maybe?'

Roberto saw the smashed jar of vinegar on the floor, looked up to see the rotting crab carcass at the back of the room, and promptly nodded his head. 'I think that probably explains it.'

Whew.

'You need to come with me,' he said. 'I've got something to show you. Where's Anna?'

'I don't know,' Maddie replied. 'I was about to go look for her. Why?'

'I'll explain on the way,' he said, pushing her out of the apartment and slamming the door behind him.

***

Lights were flashing in the hospital car park as ambulances and police cars were all bundled close together. Just as Maddie and Roberto made it there, slipping through the crowds of stressed parents with orange and blue blankets thrown over their shoulders, an armoured jeep tore around the corner and skidded over a mound of dirt, spraying them with it as it stopped beside one of the ambulances.

Six soldiers jumped out, carrying automatic rifles and covered in black, heavy-plated armour.

'What the hell is happening here?' Maddie asked.

'I told you already,' he replied. 'Exploding people. Baby crabs. I was being serious.'

'Christ.'

The soldiers all advanced on the hospital with their guns cocked and charged at the entrance. They weren't planning on heading inside, at least not yet. They just wanted to make sure that nobody was going to get out.

Roberto went ahead anyway, stopped by one of the policemen who grabbed his shoulder and told him, very firmly, that he could not enter the building.

'My wife is in there,' he said. 'She's close to the entrance. If you just let me in I can...'

'Nobody is going in there,' the man growled, a cap covering his bald head. 'Now please step away. Thank you.'

He did.

'So, this man,' said Maddie. 'He was calling Anna's name, yes?'

'Yeah,' Roberto replied. 'I thought she might know him.'

'Anna doesn't know anyone.'

'Well, this someone clearly knows her. Or did, until he...'

'Exploded.'

'Yeah.'

Maddie reached into her coat pocket and pulled out her phone. 'I'll ring her,' she said, scrolling through her contacts. 'Let's see what she's up to.'

The phone rang out, kicking her to voicemail. She tried again. Same thing. She tried a third time. No difference.

'Goddammit,' said Maddie.

'Nothing?'

'Nothing yet.'

'Keep trying,' he said. 'I'm going to get a closer look.'

He tried to dash off, but Maddie caught his right elbow, causing him to wince. 'Be careful,' she said. 'If they catch you getting too close they'll probably blast you.'

'Nay needs me,' he replied.

'I know that, just, don't be an idiot. I'm already with one of those. I need someone sensible for a change.'

Roberto didn't reply, and in the end, Maddie released him.

Trying her number again, Maddie held the phone close to her ear and cursed under her breath as it rang out, over and over again, going to voicemail every single time.

'Where the hell are you?' she whispered to herself. 'This isn't the time to be sketchy.'

Roberto, meanwhile, snuck around the outside of the hospital, always looking to keep the treeline between himself and the people that would almost definitely shoot him in the face if they saw him, and he didn't want that. Not yet.

The soldiers had fanned out a little, attempting to cover multiple exits and entrances as best as they could. South Marshwood's hospital wasn't the biggest as, well, the place itself wasn't the biggest either, but it was still a lot for only six people to deal with.

Roberto leapt from behind the cover of a tree and into one of the bushes just shy of the back entrance, before his head popped out and he looked left, then right, scuttling out of it and into the hospital. The double doors slid open on their own, leading to another set that didn't, and after he crept inside, he snuck around one of the walls and waited.

There was chatter outside, two passing soldiers making their rounds.

Roberto listened. One of them was talking about what he was going to have for dinner later, and the other clearly didn't give a shit. It sounded like he wanted a pizza, but then considered the ethical dilemma of having eaten a pizza two nights in a row, and how he just couldn't bring himself to do such a thing.

'That's great, Bob,' said the other one. 'Just keep your eyes on the door. If anyone comes through...'

'We shoot 'em,' he replied, grumpy. 'Yeah, got it.'

Roberto's desire for gossip almost kept him there to continue listening to the guy's problems, but, there were bigger ones at hand, and once their attention was elsewhere, he snuck further into the hospital. There were thin streaks of blood across the marble floor leading through the corridor, with chairs having been overturned and strewn about the place.

Coming up to where it had all kicked off, Roberto saw that the doctor – the one without any eyes – had already started to go green, but only slightly. It was a slow, gradual spread, with only a few veins plumping up around his neck.

That was good to know, as it meant Roberto still had time.

He pushed on, keeping low, watching out for any other baby crabs that might've stayed inside whilst the others were melted in the sunlight. There was a wet slap behind him, loud and close. He turned around, eyes darting all around to find where it came from, noticing, at last, that it was just the doctor's jawbone hitting the floor after it detached itself from his face.

'Nasty,' he said.

Peering through the windows, knowing he was nearby, Roberto swung around towards the front door leading into Naomi's emergency room. He wrenched the door open, stepped inside, and shut it behind him.

She was still alive in there, her heart rate monitor beeping that same, monotonous beep. Her skin had plumped up more since the last time and, after seeing what happened to Jon, he knew it was only a matter of time before she went the same way.

'Hey,' he said, sitting down beside her. 'I said I'd come back, right?'

Naomi, for obvious reasons, didn't reply.

'So, I know you probably can't hear me, and that's okay. You might not even know I'm here at all, but... Look, I have something to show you.' He slipped his admittedly torn coat off of his shoulders and placed it onto the back of his chair, rolling up his right sleeve just after. 'Snap,' he said, pointing at the small but still fatal cut that ran about halfway down his arm, with a light green tint spreading outwards across his skin.

The two of them stayed there, in silence, and waited for the end to come.

***

Meanwhile, Maddie kept calling Anna until, finally, she got an answer.

'H-Hello?' Anna mumbled, sounding faint. 'What's up?'

'Where are you?' Maddie asked. 'What's going on? There's, well, a situation at the hospital and we need you here. That guy that turned up at your door the other day? Jon? I know you won't remember his name, but he knows yours and people are looking for you. Do you know anything about that?' She paused for a moment. 'Are you there? Hello?'

'Hey...' Anna said, again. Her voice was more nasally than usual and her phone service was jittery. 'Come again?'

'Where are you?' Maddie asked, again. 'Where did you go?'

'It's a funny story,' said Anna. 'You're gonna find it funny.'

Maddie furrowed her brows. 'Try me.'

'Just promise you won't be mad.'

'Okay.'

'It's very important that you don't get mad.'

'Anna!' she barked. 'Where are you?'

CHAPTER TWENTY-ONE

GIANT CARNIVOROUS WORM

Anna woke up, eventually, with her face buried in a load of pink, sticky flesh. She pulled away from it, feeling it ping from her face like a rubber band as she stumbled backwards and onto her backside.

She looked around her. She couldn't see anything. She switched her flashlight on, and that didn't help, either. Her eyes still worked, for the most part, there just wasn't anything to see. She was in a massive, endless tunnel of skin.

'Oh,' she said, looking around, concerned, before throwing her fist in the air. 'It worked!' she cheered. 'Fuck yeah! I'm in the worm, baby! Woo!'

She bounced up and down on the spongy ground below like she was having the time of her life, and perhaps she was. This was her plan, after all, to get inside the giant worm. And now... she didn't know.

Eh, she thought. *I'm sure it'll come to me.* So, she started walking, and after a few minutes, still had nothing.

And then it had been well over an hour.

How big is this fucking thing? she thought. *I've been walking for days.*

She hadn't, but, it made sense that she thought that. The air inside the worm was heavy, and made her feel like she weighed a tonne, or that her coat had been loaded down with bricks. With that thought in mind, she emptied out her pockets.

She didn't find any bricks in there; obviously.

'George?' she called out. 'You around here, buddy?'

Nothing. She kept walking, finally coming to a change of scenery. Above her head and all around that particular area of the worm were these glowing bulbs that granted her light, warmth, and a lot of anxiety. They were very plump and bulbous, two descriptors that Anna had become far too accustomed to being able to apply things to over the last couple of days, so she didn't stick around them for long.

They were bad news, she could feel it.

'Fuck,' she panted. 'I am outta shape.'

Wanting to settle down, just for a few minutes to get her energy back, the worm had clearly gotten tired of laying around and decided to do the opposite. Seeing the tunnels wiggle back and forth ahead of and behind her, she got the sneaking suspicion that the worm was on the move again, and once she checked her own GPS location – thankful for just the single bar of signal she had left – she all but confirmed that it was.

This wasn't a big problem, but not wanting to seem like a dog in a moving vehicle, she stuck to the ground in case the ride got a bit too bumpy. Waves started rippling through the flesh of the worm as it picked up speed. Anna felt it raise up from behind, like a jet had begun its take-off procedure.

'Whoa, whoa, whoa!' she said, rolling over to cling onto some loose flaps of skin. 'Stop that, you!'

It didn't listen, still ascending, tilting her further back until the steep incline was almost vertical. She looked down, which was a mistake. Below her was just an abyss; a dark, unexplored section of the worm that probably looked identical to the light and very-much-explored sections of the worm. But still, it was a long-ass way down, and her fingers were losing their grip.

'Fuck,' she said, feeling her rucksack weigh her down. 'Fuck, fuck, fuck.'

The sweat at her fingers and the slime of the worm's insides became too much for Anna to cling onto, and as the worm tilted upwards and back onto itself, she was dangling from an overhang. She slipped, her fingernails slicing through the flesh of the worm as she slid down it for a moment, before falling.

Looking upwards as the green testicle-lamps flashed past her and the giant wall of flesh stared her in the face, whizzing by, she had an idea. An idea that she wished she'd had only five seconds earlier.

***

A full thirty seconds after that, she was still falling. The initial shock of her descent wore off eventually, and her throat was starting to ache from all the screaming, so she stopped.

Am I bored? she thought. *Is dying really this lame?*

That's when she hit the bottom, barrelling down a slope that got less and less steep as it went on before she was flung into, and swallowed whole by, a thick layer of meat.

Get out. Get out. Get out. You need to get out now. Get out. Get out. Get out.

It was one of her worst fears. She was trapped, unable to move. Her phone was ringing and she couldn't even wiggle around enough to answer it.

Anna liked to move at all times. She wanted to move at all times. She needed to move at all times because if she didn't it meant that whatever was chasing her could catch up, and there was always something chasing her.

Until next time, Annie. Closer than you think.

She had to dig her way out with just her fingernails.

Bundling up handfuls of skin and fat before tearing them apart, only for them to repair themselves and suffocate her was tiresome. She didn't open her eyes as all she could see was darkness, so what was the point? Her breath was being forced out of her as the meat squashed her chest, so her mouth was off limits, too, but she kept digging. One hand broke through the top and she was able to wiggle it around just a bit more as she pushed herself harder, kicking her feet about from under herself as she tried to swim upwards.

It was exhausting, and when she felt something squeeze itself tight around her hand again, she accepted that it was over. It'd just grown back, and she didn't have the energy to try it again.

This is not how I figured I'd go, she thought. *What a rip.*

And, as she drifted off, she thought of the man that called her here, whatever his name was. Another person she'd failed.

I'll add that one to the list.

She thought of Roberto, and his wife, who she knew probably wasn't going to make it.

Add that one, too.

And then, lastly, as she went to think of Maddie, she was hoisted out of the ground by her hand and tossed to the floor. Gasping for air, she didn't care that it tasted like shit, just that it was breathable.

'Holy fuck biscuits,' she said, jolting upwards. 'I'm alive.'

There was a figure standing over her, in the darkness, and that's when she wasn't so happy.

Oh, fuck, she thought. *It can't be. He's not real. He's just a dream. He can't get me here.*

Closer than you think, Annie.

Anna whipped out her flashlight and shone it into the man's face, seeing that – after close inspection – it was just some guy.

'I found you,' the man said. 'Oh, thank god.'

He took Anna by the hand and pulled her to her feet.

'I'm Geoff,' he said. 'You're Anna, right? Anna Pendleton?'

'Sure am,' she replied. 'You're the guy on the phone, yeah?'

'That's me,' he smiled, before he leant down and spat a huge wad of blood onto the floor. 'That's me.'

Eww, that's gross as fuck, Anna thought but didn't say. *Be nice. He saved your life.*

'I need to get out of this thing,' said Geoff, grabbing Anna by the shoulders and shaking her. 'Y-You can help me, right?'

'I'll try my best,' she replied, pushing him away as his bloodshot eyes and loose skin made her feel nauseous. 'It's lucky you pulled me outta there, mate. We'd have both been fucked, otherwise.'

Geoff nodded. 'But, that does mean you're now down here, too. Trapped. Like me.'

'Don't stress it,' said Anna, removing her rucksack. 'Here, take this.'

She tossed him a bottle of water, and Geoff had finished the whole thing before she could even tell him that he absolutely should not do that.

'W-W-What's the plan?' Geoff asked. 'You have a plan, right?'

'Sure do.'

Barely.

'It's a great plan.'

It wasn't.

'Bound to work.'

Not even close.

'Okay,' said Geoff. 'What is it?'

Anna reached into her bag and pulled out a meat cleaver. 'We're gonna cut the bastard open.'

There was a pause. Geoff didn't look impressed.

'Good luck with that,' he said. 'You won't be getting through the wall with that.'

'Oh yeah?' she said, confidently, remembering how even just her fingernails had managed to do the job. 'Watch this.'

She wound her arm back, holding the meat cleaver over her head before she swung it down and went to split the inner walls of the worm wide open, so she could wrench a giant hole in it, drag the both of them safety, and claim her swift and easy victory.

That didn't happen. The cleaver was completely worthless, getting stuck in the wall and then popping itself out a second later without a shred of damage done.

'I don't understand,' she said. 'The walls are thin, aren't they?'

'Maybe up there,' said Geoff, pointing upwards into the endless chasm above their heads. 'But, the flesh down here is thick. That's how come you got stuck in the stuff. It's... thicker, somehow.'

'Up there?' Anna snapped. 'Where the fuck are we?'

'This is the bottom of the worm,' he said. 'God knows how far you'd have to go to get to the top again. I dread to think.'

'Oh, shit.'

'So, I take it that was your plan?'

Anna didn't respond to that. She was too busy feeling like a twat.

'Well, you might as well come and have a sit-down,' he said, walking towards the back wall where a droopy ceiling lamp hung in the middle of a smaller, cave-like segment. 'Make yourself at home. What's mine is yours.' He looked her dead in the eye. 'I don't have anything.'

'Shit,' said Anna, her face sinking into her hands. 'Shit!'

'Oh, just a heads up,' Geoff went on. 'That thing up there,' he pointed to the green, pulsating light above them. 'That thing's getting ready to burst, and when it does, we'll have a crawler on our hands. You're welcome to try and kill it, but if you could let it tear my head off before you do I'd really appreciate it.'

'The crabs come from here?' she asked. 'Interesting.'

Geoff didn't respond. Instead, he laid down on the floor and curled up into a ball, coughing and spluttering blood into his sweat-soaked polo shirt.

'A crawler?' Anna whispered to herself. 'That's a much better name, holy shit.'

The air was already taking its toll on her. Geoff was right. It truly was toxic and her lungs were struggling. Anna's phone buzzed, and – before she could fall down – she gently eased herself onto the ground and answered it.

'H-H-Hello?'

CHAPTER TWENTY-TWO

BREAKOUT

Anna waited a long time before giving Maddie an answer. So long, in fact, that one presented itself to them in the form of a giant carnivorous worm.

The ground shook violently, throwing Maddie off balance and letting the phone slip from her hand, skidding across the concrete and hitting the curb beside her. The police cars all started firing their sirens off and their headlights flashed as windows were blown out and tires burst.

Those gathered around, still in shock from the baby crab attack, were tossed about the place as they tried to hang on. Some were lucky, grabbing ahold of car doors or trees or each other, but some weren't so much. One man who'd been clutching an orange pillow close to his chest for the last hour was thrown to the ground, slamming his head into the ambulance loading ramp so hard that it ripped the top few inches off.

His brain slipped out onto the floor in a pool of blood, and that's when the screaming really started.

Maddie crawled on her hands and knees to her phone and picked it up, seeing another crack down the screen before placing it to her head. 'What's happening?' she said. 'Jesus, it's chaos out here. Are you still there? Please, tell me you're okay.'

A few blocks over in the centre of the south forest, a large clump of trees were sucked underground as another sinkhole opened, spraying chunks of dirt and wood high into the air. Maddie looked over towards it, eyes ready to fall out of her skull as she saw something glistening in the moonlight. The silhouette shot up well over a hundred feet above the treeline.

'Oh, Christ,' said Maddie. 'What is it now?'

The monster roared; a noise heard even by Roberto as it shattered the last of the windows left standing in the hospital. Maddie covered her ears, but it did little good. The sound pierced right through.

'Anna!' yelled Maddie, half-deaf as she held her phone up to her face. 'Please don't tell me you're inside that bloody thing.'

There was a pause.

'Maybe,' Anna replied, drawing out the word.

'Oh, for Christ's sake. You're an idiot.'

'Yeah.'

'What do we do?'

'I dunno,' said Anna.

'You always know.'

'Not this time.'

'Don't say that now.'

'I can say it later if you'd like?'

'Shut up. This is serious,' said Maddie, taking a deep breath. 'Just, focus with me, yeah?'

Anna stared down at her feet, digging her heels into the worm's thick skin. She was ready to pack it in. It'd been a long, long day, but Maddie's voice, no matter how unclear it

142 · THOMAS E. STAPLES

was, made her feel alright again. If there was any time to be an annoying, energetic little shit, it was now.

'Okay,' Anna said, with a smile. 'Let's think. What's happening out there?'

The worm sunk back out of sight, taking half a dozen more trees with it along the way.

'Big worm,' she said, 'disconcertingly big. It's just gone back underground. It's off under the forest somewhere by the looks of it. Probably in the sewer system. What's happening in there?'

'Big worm,' Anna repeated. 'Obviously. I'm stuck in here with some guy, Greg or George or Gary or something.'

'It's none of those, is it?'

'Probably not. But that ain't all. There are these glowing egg-looking things. It's where the crabs come from. I can see it twitching in there. Big fucker, too, and...'

There was a long silence.

'And?' asked Maddie.

'Hang on,' said Anna. 'I'm cross-referencing.'

'What? What does that even mean?'

'I dunno.'

'How can you not know?'

'My finger birthed one of those crab things, right?' said Anna. 'It was infected, so a baby one popped out. They're breeding that way.'

'Go on...'

'What if it wasn't a baby, though? What if it was... I dunno... a test?'

'I'm lost.'

Anna paced up and down the inside of the worm, picking at her chin.

'Stop slapping yourself,' said Maddie. 'I forbid it.'

'I'm not.'

'I can hear you doing it.'

'It helps me focus,' she said, defensively. 'But listen, that baby crab in the apartment was weak. It wasn't just young, it was barely functioning at all.'

'So?'

'So, maybe this worm is the next step up. You know how a gross looking caterpillar turns into a not-as-gross but still kinda gross looking butterfly?'

'Sure,' Maddie replied, only just grasping it. 'But what makes you think that?'

'Because I've licked both of them.'

Her head sank into her hands. 'Of course you have.'

'Anyway, the crab is the caterpillar, and the worm is...'

'The butterfly,' said Maddie.

'Exactly! But that takes ages, so, the crabs have tried skipping the queue by producing young earlier; using our delicious, meaty faces as a host. Evidently, it's not going so well. They're weak and, well, just a bit shit, really, but they're gonna keep trying.'

'Now that you mention it,' added Maddie. 'Roberto said that a bunch of the little ones attacked him, but the sunlight just killed them outright.'

'Bingo,' said Anna. 'They can't even go outside. Their bodies can't take it.'

'So, what are you doing to do?'

'I'm gonna kill this fat fucker,' Anna replied. 'Just, keep people away from any and all crab-monsters.'

'How are you going to do that?'

'Dunno yet, but, hey, you know me,' she said, jumping up. 'Fuck, now this shit is exciting. Isn't it exciting? Aren't you excited?'

'I'm tepid,' replied Maddie. 'Just don't die, please.'

'Well, I wasn't planning on it,' she said. 'I'll be fine. I'm a tough cookie, remember? I'm like Mike Tyson, baby. I fly like a pigeon, and fuck like a badger.'

Maddie's jaw fell open. 'I can't even begin to describe all of the things you got wrong just then.'

'Yeah, yeah, whatever. Remember, keep everyone away from the south bridge. Don't just let some random fucker sneak his way past because he'll be dead as shit by the morning, 'kay?'

'Okay.'

'Okay,' said Anna. 'Speak soon.'

'I love you,' Maddie said, quickly, but not quick enough, as Anna had already hung up.

She turned around to find that the armoured car had gone, so she ran over to all of the battered cars and angry looking policeman, spotting one in particular – the same one that stopped Roberto earlier – and tapped him on the shoulder.

'Where did all your men go?' she asked, seeing that the soldiers that surrounded the hospital were nowhere to be found.

'They've been sent to tackle a larger threat,' the man replied, barely paying attention to her. 'They'll be back once that's been taken care of, don't worry yourself.'

'The giant worm?' Maddie asked. 'You need to bring them back. It's not safe out there.'

'Yes, ma'am. That's why they have guns.'

'But...'

'Listen,' he said, suddenly giving her his full, visibly irritated attention. 'They're doing a helluva lot more out there than they would here, and in the interest of minimizing civilian casualties, it's best to tackle the problem at the source. That clear?'

It was, but Maddie didn't like it. She'd been given one job to do, but, how could she explain herself? *My friend's inside of that thing,* she thought of saying. *Just let her do it all on her own and everything'll be hunky-dory.*

It was stupid. Maddie would never say hunky-dory.

'Fine,' she said. 'As you were.'

The man just grunted as she backed away. Maybe he was right, after all. Anna would always reject help; she knew that. Maybe she just didn't want anyone stealing her thunder, and besides, they were equipped well enough to take on anything that came their way, as long as they saw it coming.

And therein lied the problem.

They were never going to see it coming.

CHAPTER TWENTY-THREE

WHEN THE NIGHT COMES

The six soldiers couldn't see shit without their gun-mounted flashlights as they trudged through the forest, crunching leaves and snapping fallen branches as they pushed towards the sinkhole, so they all stuck close together with weapons at the ready.

Morale was still high with Gus as their leader. Bob was still thinking about his pizza, and Gareth was still busy not giving a shit about any of it. With visibility so low they kept chatter to a similar standard, only speaking when absolutely necessary.

'God, I'm hungry,' said Bob. 'Anyone else hungry?'

They all either snarled, ignored him, or told him to eat a dick.

'Rude.'

It didn't take long to find the sinkhole and have it surrounded on all sides. One of the soldiers shone his flashlight directly into it, unable to see all the way down, finding a bunch of torn up roots as they sprinkled more dirt down into the darkness instead.

'You see anything?' Bob asked him, standing a foot or two to his left.

'Nope,' Gus replied, his voice slightly muffled by his mask. 'Have a look, would ya? I gotta go for a piss.'

'Oh, well, the truck's only a couple minutes away,' he said. 'It'd probably be safer to do it there, where you can see.'

'Nah, fuck that. I ain't walking all that way.'

'You locked it, right?'

'Yeah, course,' he said. 'Back in a sec.'

Gus took a step back and walked off into the dark to find a suitable tree to relieve himself onto, away from all the others, whilst Bob had a gander inside the sinkhole. He shuffled closer, but not too close. He wasn't looking to fall in, and any slight noise was making him jump out of his skin, even when his own stomach rumbled, which it did all the damn time.

'Anyone else see anything?' Bob asked. 'Anything at all?'

A series of different sounding grunts was the only reply he got.

'Okay,' he said. 'Good to know.'

Some slight chatter was murmuring amongst the troops – none of it involving Bob of course, as it never did – until the team decided it would soon be time to press on.

'Alright,' said Bob, turning around. 'Goddamn, dude. How long does it take to pee?'

He lifted his rifle to shine a light over to where he assumed Gus would be, finding his body slumped against the tree with his stomach pulled inside out and splattered across the ground.

'Oh, fuck!' he shouted. 'Guys!'

A flurry of lights all converged on Gus' mutilated body, bouncing off of one of the crabs as it scratched his ribcage clean. Knowing it'd been spotted, the crab shot up the tree and out of sight before they could open fire.

'Shit,' said Bob, turning to his squad. 'Do we fall back?'

148 · THOMAS E. STAPLES

He was looking to Gareth for an answer, seeing that there was another large crab-monster where his buddy's head was supposed to be. He was still screaming under there, whatever was left of him, as the toothy underbelly of the crab had wrapped itself around his head and started munching through his neck. He screamed for help and for someone to do something, anything at all, but it was too late. Gareth fired his rifle off a few times as his limbs twitched, sending a series of rounds into a nearby tree and blowing a few chunks of bark off of it before he – along with the crab – tumbled into the sinkhole.

'They're above us!' another man shouted, as their flash-light caught a glimpse of a crab's underside before it fell onto his head and split him straight down the middle.

Bob fired a few shots at another one as it scuttled through the grass, chasing a soldier that'd already bailed, leaving his gun in the dirt. He made it a few feet, passing behind a tree, before a giant claw slammed straight through it, dripping with blood and the poor bastard's heart stuck on the end of it. The claw retracted with a wet pop and the crab sunk its mandibles into the guy's face, peeling it off.

Bob ran, too. He knew there was one other member of his squad that just might have made it out alive, but there was no time to check.

The armoured truck wasn't far ahead, he remembered saying that, so he kept running. Clearing out of the treeline as the grass was shredded by skittering claws and snapping mandibles, Bob was only slowed when he crashed into the door of the truck. He reached into his pocket, fishing for the keys.

He didn't have them. Of course he didn't have them. Why would he?

He turned around. A dozen crabs had surrounded him on all sides, some with blood oozing from their mouths, itching for about eight pints more. He raised his gun and sent a few shots straight ahead, bouncing bullets off of their armoured backs and doing almost nothing to them. One shot came right back for him, whizzing past his ear and pelting the window of the armoured truck, putting a slight crack in it.

The car alarm, however, didn't sound.

'Oh, for fuck sake, Gus,' said Bob. 'You fucking idiot.'

He spun around and wrenched the truck door open, which was, of course, completely unlocked, and had been for a while now. Slamming the door behind him, one of the crabs leapt and stuck a claw into the metal, piercing a hole right through it and skimming Bob's leg.

He squeaked, looking around to see that the keys were in the ignition.

'You beautiful fucking idiot.'

He turned it and the engine fired up. The headlights were on full blast, lighting up the dark country road ahead. A crash came above him. Bob looked at it.

'Oh, shit,' he said, as the sound of more crab-like feet clambering over metal circled around the truck. 'Oh, shit.'

The door flew open on the passenger side.

Oh, no, he thought. *They can open doors, too.*

It wasn't a crab. It was the only other survivor of Bob's team, and he was plastered head to toe in blood.

'Shut the fucking door!' Bob yelled.

He did.

'Good! We're getting the fuck out of here!'

The engine roared as Bob slammed his foot down on the pedal, one of the tires spraying green blood up the road after a crab tried to wedge itself under the tires. The truck pulled away, and as Bob focused his eyes on the road ahead of him, one of the bastards landed on the bonnet and started snapping its claws outside of the windshield.

'Fuck off!' Bob yelled, behind his bulletproof glass. 'You ain't coming in!'

The crab stuck its sharp, underslung fingers through the windshield and ripped it off in one, clean piece, before tossing it off into a nearby ditch.

'Okay,' said Bob. 'That's bad.'

He reached down to his belt, one hand still on the wheel, before pulling up his sidearm, flicking the safety off, and popping the crab in the face with a couple of quick shots. Its many eyes burst as he hit the weak spot, spraying eye-juice into his face before it slipped off to the side and got ground up under the wheels.

'That was close, eh?' he said, not turning to the man next to him, who was still frozen against the passenger seat, stiff as a board.

Bob breathed a heavy sigh, relieved, just for a moment before the roof was torn off.

'Oh, knackers,' Bob yelled. 'Watch out!'

A spindly hand came down into the top of the passenger's head,where it crawled along his face like a bug and stuck its fingers into his neck, tearing his head off and chomping it down between its jaws. Blood squirted out of the man's neck hole like a geyser and the crab leapt away onto the spare tire at the back, munching away at the rear window.

'Fuck arse.'

Bob looked up, seeing six more eyes staring back at him, and sent a couple of rounds upwards, blowing out his own eardrums. The crab fell down into the car, dazed, and Bob quickly shimmied it off of himself and onto his dead passenger's lap. Throwing the door on the other side open, he kicked that crab out and carried on driving, seeing the hospital in the distance with god knows how many more following close behind.

***

Maddie was sat on the curb, waiting. In the meantime, someone had been kind enough to toss a blanket over the nearly headless corpse from earlier. It was still obvious what it was, with blood spilling around the edges, but after one too many people stood in the chunks of brain and slipped over it seemed like the suitable thing to do.

Most of them had gone home, too, but not everyone. People without anyone to give them a lift home or those without a home to go to were left out in the dark, to the mercy of whatever monsters lurked in the forest.

So, Maddie stayed.

There were lights in the distance. Maddie looked up as they got closer, before they came to a halt, skidding across the road and slamming into the side of the ambulance no-one had gone near since the accident.

Bob hopped out, screaming his head off, which was luckily still on for the time being.

'JESUS FUCK!' he yelled, with his rifle in one hand and a crab hot on his tail. 'HELP ME YOU BASTARD!'

He was referring to the sergeant who, after getting bored a few minutes ago, left to go for a coffee and a quick wee.

Maddie leapt up instead. 'Pass it here!' she yelled back, and Bob hurled his rifle over to her. She caught it by the barrel, flicked the rifle around, and pressed the stock against her shoulder.

She crouched down and aimed with both eyes open. A bullet came whizzing through Bob's legs and knocked the crab flat on its back. He let out a high-pitch squeal when he processed how close he came to losing his testicles, and then a much lower one when he realised he still had them.

Maddie marched over to the crab as it thrashed about on the ground, kicking out with all of its limbs and trying to right itself. She shot it in the belly and burst it wide open, its blood spilling out onto the floor.

'You good?' she said, gun-in-hand.

'Everyone's dead,' he replied, sweating, pointing to the car that was still occupied by his headless passenger. 'There were thousands of 'em. We couldn't see them coming.'

'Thousands?'

'Yeah!' he said. 'Well, no, like ten, but that's still a lot!'

'Where are they now?'

'Well, they're...'

The two went silent as their heads slowly turned towards the armoured truck, sitting still in the dark. There were no crabs in sight, as far as they could see.

'The other rifle is in there,' Bob whispered. 'I need to get it back if more show up.'

'Then let's get on it, shall we?' she asked. 'I'll cover you.'

'I-I'd feel safer if I had the gun.'

Maddie glared at him. 'That's a shame,' she said.

The two approached the truck, Bob standing only a couple of metres ahead of Maddie, as he reached out to pull the door open. The headless soldier was still holding his rifle, tight, so Bob had to wrestle with it to try and pry the fingers away.

It wasn't working.

'Come on, ye bastard,' he said. 'I'll get the knife.'

'Hurry up,' she said, looking up and down the empty, poorly lit street.

'I'm working on it.' He took his knife out and jimmied the rifle from the man's dead fingers. 'Sorry, buddy.'

Just as he'd got it, a crab leapt up onto the roof of the truck – well, what was left of it – and screamed in Bob's pale, terrified looking face. Its fingers fluttered with sharp nails at the ready, until Maddie shot its face right off, knocking it the ground where it staggered around for a bit. They all watched it, amused, as it tried to find its balance with blood spurting out of the front before it crashed headfirst into a dustbin and bled to death.

'Have you got a spare magazine?' Maddie asked. 'This one's dry.'

'Sure,' said Bob, reaching into his bag and handing one over. 'Oh, to reload it you need to...'

Maddie popped the magazine out and had a new one loaded in and ready to fire before the first had hit the floor. 'All good,' she said. 'Let's get ready. There might be more coming.'

***

Even after the first gunshot, Roberto hadn't moved from his wife's side. He'd thought about it, yes, but, he hadn't gone beyond that. But then there was another shot, and another, and another. It became harder to stay put; to do nothing.

Don't get involved, he thought. *Your place is here.*

'I'm not sure how long this is going to take,' he said, looking at his infected arm. 'It could be a while, so—'

Gunshots.

'But anyway,' he went on, trying to distract himself. 'I was thinking...'

More gunshots.

'I was thinking that...'

Even more, closer together this time; multiple guns firing at once.

'Goddammit,' he said, standing up and peeking out of the doorway into the car park.

There were flashes of light. A soldier was out there trying to shuffle people to safety. Maddie was there, too, kicking crabs across the concrete and shooting them in the belly. And Roberto, well, he was inside.

He wasn't doing anything.

'You know what, Nay?' he said, poking his head into the emergency room. 'I'll be right back.'

CHAPTER TWENTY-FOUR

THERE AIN'T NO MOUNTAIN HIGH ENOUGH

'Come on,' said Anna, kicking Geoff up the backside. 'We're getting outta here, right now. Move your shit and let's get crackin'. We gotta long way to go.'

'Leave me alone,' he groaned, the air of the worm further rotting his brain. 'We aren't getting out of here.'

'Oh, what's that?' she said, cupping her ear. 'I think that's the sound of a *massive* pussy, that's what that is.'

He sat up. 'You cannot get out of the worm down here. It's too thick. We might as well be in a concrete tube.'

'Down here, maybe,' Anna reminded him. 'But up there its thinner, like you said. I felt it myself before I fell, even my nails managed to scrape through it, and look at them!' she held her fingers up and waited for him to look.

He didn't.

'They're practically down to the bone,' she said. 'Imagine what we can do with this fucker.' She held out her cleaver and did some slashing motions. 'And this thing chops through bone real good.'

She was going to show off her missing finger, but she knew he wasn't going to give a shit, so she didn't.

'Okay,' he said, 'but you're still down here. You'd need to be at the top. Slice through the belly.'

'Do worms have bellies?'

'Does it matter?'

'Not really.'

'Wonderful.'

'And so what that we're down here?' she said. 'We'll just have ourselves a road trip. It's a long way, sure, but we'll get there.'

'I'm nearly fifty,' he replied. 'And I'm tired. I can barely see. I feel like my brain is going to fall out.'

'Oh, hold on a second,' she whispered, cupping her ear again. 'That pussy's back again. If we just ignore it, it might go away.'

'You know, you're a real arsehole.'

'Hey!' said Anna. 'Don't gimme that shit. I came in here to save you, remember?'

'Oh yeah?' he replied, lying back down. 'I'm sure the idea of a cash reward had nothing to do with it at all, right?'

She didn't reply to that.

'Who the hell prints that on a business card, anyway?' he said, sitting back up. 'You're selfish.'

'Y'know, a lot of people have told me that. It's crazy.'

'Probably because it's true. I called your number six times before I got an answer from you. Were you concerned at all, or were you too busy doing god knows what people your age get up to?'

Anna didn't reply to that, either. If she'd have told him why she didn't answer the phone, then, he'd have really thought she was a piece of shit and she wasn't a piece of shit.

Right?

'If you want to get out of here, then fine, take your little butcher knife and go cut your way out on your own, but when this thing rears its head and you come tumbling back down here, don't expect me to pull your arse out of the ground again.'

He pressed his head tightly into his hands. Anna stared at the floor, her face a bright red as her heart raced. It was a strange feeling, it wasn't excitement, but more so the opposite.

She felt like she was dying. She wanted to apologise.

That's something people do, right?

'I didn't mean that,' he groaned, looking up. 'I'm in a bad mood.'

'Right.'

'I was just told that you would be able to help me. They gave me your email and said that was all I needed. I feel gipped.'

Anna took a step back. 'Who told you that?' she asked.

'Huh?'

'Who gave you my details?'

'Oh, just some guy,' he said.

'Some guy? What guy?'

'Just some guy!' he shouted, spitting blood. 'I don't know, lady. I was in my house, and then this big thing came up from under it and swallowed me whole. I died, sort of, and then this guy appeared and gave me *your* information. I don't re-member what he said after that.'

'Gregory...' she said, skin as pale as it'd ever been.

'Geoffrey,' he corrected her, 'my name is Geoffrey.'

'Did you just say that you...'

'Died?' said Geoff, completely casual as if it weren't a big deal. 'Well, yeah, of course I did. At least, I think so.'

'Then how am I talking to you right now?'

'Well because I...' His eyes looked ready to pop out. 'I-I-I don't remember.'

'What did this man look like?' said Anna. 'Describe him to me.'

'I don't remember.'

'TRY TO!' she screamed. 'Please!'

Geoff saw the frightened look on her face and gave himself a moment. He closed his eyes and looked all around his brain, trying to recall exactly what'd happened that night.

He remembered the business card. He remembered that he should've died. He remembered a figure, made entirely of shadow with a hideous fucking face and... a message.

Three words. Three letters for three words.

'F.A.P.' said Geoff. 'F.A.P.'

'What were those words?' Anna asked, rushing over to the old man. 'I need to know. What were they?'

Geoff scrunched his eyes up tight, his fists trembling as he tried to see past the rot in his brain. He opened his eyes. They were bleeding, as were his nose and ears and... just about everything else.

He met her gaze up close, pushed his teeth together and whispered. 'Find Anna Pendleton.'

Those were Geoff's last words before his lifeless body hit the floor.

'Hello?' said Anna. 'You still with me, buddy?'

She felt for his pulse, just as she'd seen Maddie do, and found nothing. She stumbled backwards, feeling jittery, more so than usual, which was saying something. Her lips vibrated as she scratched lines down her face. She pulled at her short, sticky hair until a few more ginger strands came away, stuck to her fingers.

'Okay,' she said, struggling to get the word out. 'Okay, okay, okay. Shit.'

She took a deep breath, looked up at the lamp above her, and then the endless darkness just beyond that. It was flat which meant, were she quick enough, she might've been able to run to the top of the worm and carve her way out of its weak belly.

Anna was not that quick.

So, she waited, patiently, and closed her eyes. When she opened them again the worm was upright, seemingly going upwards forever. Maddie was standing beside her, and after a nod, ran towards the wall and started to climb it. She got a little way with her fingers, but the stiffness of the worm's flesh didn't let her get a good enough grip, so she slid back down, got stuck, and suffocated.

'Fuck,' said Anna, hands shaking. 'Come on.'

She looked to her left and Maddie was there again. Her expression was blank as, of course, she wasn't really there. Maddie took a cleaver out of thin air and used that to scale the wall, wedging it in horizontally and heaving herself upwards until she could get a grip with her fingers, and again with the blade; rinse and repeat.

She got a little further, an extra dozen feet or so, but the cleaver was too sharp and clean, slipping out of the wall. Maddie fell, slid back down, got stuck, and suffocated.

'Almost there,' Anna whispered, picking at her chin. 'I'm closer than...'

Closer than you think?

'Shut up, brain.'

She closed her eyes, tight, and then opened them. The worm was lying flat again, Maddie was gone, and she had an idea. The bulbous lamp above her head was glowing brighter than ever, and inside it sat one of the crabs, huddled into a ball as it shook the egg sac.

It was getting ready to hatch.

'I ain't got time for your shit,' she said, to the ball. 'I'm gonna wake you a bit early if that's cool?'

This is a bad idea. This is a bad idea. This is a bad idea.

She took out her cleaver and hurled it at the egg, clipping it across the side and splitting it open. Green liquid came gushing out of it, splattering over Geoff's corpse as Anna picked her knife back up. The crab fell shortly after, unrolled itself, and shook the rest of the fluid off.

Without any light left in the room, Anna took out her flashlight and made some of her own. She shone it on the crab.

It saw her. It snapped its claws. It was pissed.

Go for the weak spots, Maddie had said, as the crab's eyes flickered individually of one another. *Go for the weak spots.*

Anna raised the cleaver above her head. The crab screeched in return, making a dash for her. Overzealous, the crab leapt in the air to hit her dead on, and Anna did the opposite, sliding underneath and catching it on the belly. She spun around, ready for another strike, to find the crab's guts spilling out and onto the floor; defeated.

'Oh, my god,' said Anna. 'I KICK ASS! WOO! FUCK YEAH! MIKE TYSON, BABY!'

She still didn't even know who that was.

Wasting no time, she flipped the crab over, holding the end of a claw in one hand and her cleaver in the other, before bringing the latter against the former. It took a few hits, but she managed to break one of the claws off, careful to not cut her hands open on the sharp ridges. The second claw came off much easier, and after that, she had a pair of three-foot-long spears.

Sharp, but not too sharp. The perfect climbing tool.

'I'm coming for ya, big boy,' she said, looking straight ahead, off into the distance, before setting off towards the top of the worm. 'I'm so never saying that again.'

***

The top of the worm was a lot easier to get to when the top of the worm actually meant the front of the worm, but when the top of the worm – which was the front of the worm – became the actual top of the worm, the top of the worm became harder to get to.

Anna had covered a lot of ground when it finally started to tip. The bottom of the worm felt like a long way away, a fall that would almost certainly get her stuck, and if she got stuck she would die.

With the worm as large as it was, Anna had a minute to prepare once it started ascending. She ran. It was much easier than climbing was going to be and she knew that, so she got as far as she could until the ground wasn't stable anymore. Upright, she felt herself slipping backwards, and shoved the claws into the wall. They stuck nicely, but the wall was still too thick.

'Oh, fuckin' shitty titties,' she said, as her legs dangled free underneath her. 'Just don't look down this time, yeah? Ya fuckin' idiot.'

She hoisted her right arm up and stuck the claw in the wall, tugged on it to check it was stable, and then did the same with the other one.

'Easy,' she said, already out of breath. 'Easy peasy. Fuck, I'm outta shape.'

She kept climbing, using the exact same technique over and over again as the wall got ever so slightly thinner with every metre cleared.

'Come on, you bastard,' she said, her arms aching. 'You got this. This wall ain't shit.'

She kept climbing...

'Imma slice this fucker open so bad.'

And climbing...

'It's gonna be so pissed.'

And climbing...

'I'll be like Zorro sliding down a curtain.'

And climbing...

'Then I'll fuck all the bitches.'

And climbing, until she hit a snag.

She'd reached the wall of flesh's awkward phase, where it was too thin to climb up without her claws sliding down a little, and too thick to truly get a good tear going. When she first realised this, one of her claws slipped out of the wall and was nearly dropped entirely, but she dealt with it, calmly, and professionally.

'Fuck, fuck, fuck, shit, arse, fuck, bollocks, wank, fuck!'

She steadied herself and jammed it back into the wall, twisting it this time to build up some flesh around the claws, helping hold her weight.

'There we go!' she cheered. 'New tactic, baby. Let's fucking go.'

She kept fucking going.

'This ain't beating me.'

And going...

'I'll climb any mountain.'

And going...

'I'm like that gay Martin guy,' she said. 'Ain't no mountain high enough for me.'

And going...

'Actually,' she said, hoarse and struggling to breath 'This is high enough.'

Then she stopped.

Jabbing at the wall with her finger, it came away like tissue paper, taking a moment to repair itself. She was right near the top. She'd made it.

'Okay,' she said, sticking one of the claws deep into the wall and out the other side. 'Let's see you heal from this, you fucker.'

She tossed the other claw away – not looking as it plummeted into the depths – and with both hands tightly wrapped around the one stuck in the wall, she kicked off with her feet and used her dead weight to pull it down.

It kept going, and going, and going.

She cheered the whole way down.

CHAPTER TWENTY-FIVE

DAMBUSTERS

The crabs scuttled towards the hospital car park en masse, filling the streets with their many arms, legs, and eyeballs once Maddie opened fire.

After Bob had shoed people backwards, away from the road, Maddie had grabbed a bag of ammo and hurled it on-top of the parked ambulance, standing up there herself for a better vantage point to take pot shots at anything with more than four legs.

And there were a lot of those.

Bob stayed on the ground, keeping an eye on the civilians, of which there were about two dozen. 'Stay here!' he called out to the huddled crowd of men, women, and children. 'Everything will be fine! There is no need to panic!'

'Jesus Christ!' yelled Maddie, a few feet away. 'There's an absolute tonne of them.'

Bob bit into his gums. 'I'll be right back,' he said, gently, before running to give her a hand. 'What's the situ—holy shit there's like fifty of 'em.'

'Sure is,' said Maddie, lining up her shot with the help of the flashlight. 'Remember, aim for the weak spots. The face, the little arms, and if you can manage it, their bellies.'

She pulled the trigger and the crab at the front lost its face. Her aim snapped between any that she caught sight of, promptly obliterating them with the gunfire. She'd take out half a dozen of them, reload, and then repeat.

Her aim was always spot on. She was good. She was almost too good.

One of the crabs made it past Maddie's defensive line as they started to bunch up together more, dividing her attention, and rammed itself into the side of the ambulance. It rocked, and Maddie almost slipped, catching her footing just before she would've tripped over the edge.

'Watch out!' she yelled. 'They're getting through.'

Metal was shoved and torn apart as the same crab dragged its way up the side of the ambulance, launching itself in the air high above Maddie, ready to drop right on her head. So she stuck her gun up in the air, held the trigger down for a second, and smirked as the crab's armoured plating spun out and stuck itself in the bonnet; hollowed out by her bullets.

'Bugger me,' said Bob, who saw it all happen. 'Why am I even here? What's the point?'

The herd had been thinned out considerably, with only a few crabs left knocking about, trying to hide behind any and all cover they could find. It didn't do much. Maddie searched them out, and when she found them, she blew them to bits.

'Is that all of them?' she said. 'You see any more?'

'Don't think so.' Bob looked around. 'I think you got 'em all.'

'Right,' said Maddie. 'Thank god for that, because I'm almost out.'

She looked towards the back of the ambulance, ready to jump off, when two pairs of tiny hands slithered up the side of it. She took aim, finger on the trigger, and was knocked flying when the crab threw itself into her.

She hit the concrete, hard. Her ears rung like she'd been hit with a flashbang as her vision suffered the same fate.

'What happened?' she heard Bob say. 'Where'd you go?'

The blurred shape in-front of Maddie was getting bigger, snapping and clicking and screeching as it prepared for its meal. It'd earned it, after all. It was the last crab standing.

Maddie panicked. She could hit anything, but not when she couldn't see more than an inch in front of her face. She sat up. It hurt like hell. Then she felt something behind her, too, gripping onto her shoulders. It was human, so, that was something. Human arms hooked around her own, pulling her backwards along the concrete.

Maddie looked up. It was Roberto. She rubbed her eyes, let her vision settle, and reached down for her rifle, pointing it into the crab's face as it tried to shield itself. It hopped backwards on top of the ambulance, saw that Bob was wandering about gormlessly, and made a go for him instead.

He was on the other side of the armoured truck, and as the crab followed after him, Maddie couldn't get a clear shot.

'Let go,' she said. 'Now.'

Roberto did as he was told, releasing his hold on her so she could move freely. She laid down, face pressed against the tarmac as she lined up her shot, aiming under the car. It was still too low for a critical hit on the crab, but that was okay. She wanted to hit the concrete.

She waited – saw legs scuttling around behind the truck as Bob bumbled his way backwards – and fired. The crab's front end was blown clean off, spraying chunks of flesh across the road as it wandered into it and a passing car smashed it to pieces. The driver stopped the car, peered out of the door, and caught a quick glimpse of what he'd just run over.

'Oh, fuck that noise,' he said, slamming the door again and gunning the car off into the distance.

'HOLY SHIT, LADY!' Bob yelled, singing a very different tune. 'Did you just do what I think you just did?'

'Depends,' Maddie groaned, not nearly as excited. 'You can help me up now. Thank you.'

Roberto did as he was told then, too, and she wrapped her arms around him to keep herself upright.

'You cannot tell Anna about this,' she said, kicking her gun away. 'Please.'

'S-Sure,' he replied, nodding, lifting her onto the curb. 'Your... talent is safe with me.'

'DID YOU BOUNCE THAT SHOT OFF OF THE FUCKING GROUND?' Bob yelled. 'HOLY SHIT!'

'That goes for you, too!' Maddie called back. 'Don't mention this to anyone, okay?'

'Oh, yeah, sure thing, lady,' Bob replied, rushing over all giddy. 'Holy shit.'

'Make sure everyone's okay.'

'Will do, boss,' said Bob. He gave a quick salute and rushed over to the group of civilians, all huddled together.

Roberto helped Maddie gain her balance. 'Can you stand?' he asked.

'I think so,' she said. 'Thank you. It's good to see you're still with us.'

'For now,' he replied. 'Are we safe now?'

'Well, that was my last shot. So, as long as we don't run into anything else, we should be fine.'

The ground tore open in full view of everyone, and the giant worm shot up a few hundred feet in the sky, roaring and thrashing about as the earth shook.

'Right,' said Roberto, staring up at it. 'That's not what I was hoping for.'

'Oh, balls.'

The worm's attention, however, seemed elsewhere, as it screamed into the sky and its fat body shrunk and grew in size.

'Come on, Anna,' Maddie whispered, fists tightly clenched. 'Do your thing. Something. Anything at all.'

A huge waterfall of blood came gushing out of the worm's fat belly in a straight line as its stomach was torn open from the inside. Anna was in there, sailing down the wall of flesh with the claw slicing straight through it, making even the thickest parts of the wall fall apart with ease, like a pair of scissors through wrapping paper. She kept going as the worm screamed and tried to fling her away from the wall, but it wasn't happening, and the wound stretched to over a hundred feet long.

'We should stand back,' said Maddie, urgently. 'Like, right now.'

'Everyone move!' Bob yelled. 'Back away!'

The worm reared its head forward and then upright, splitting its belly wide open and launching chunks of meat out onto the road. A slab of flesh the size of an elephant slammed into the ambulance and crushed it flat, all while green blood splattered the street, the cars and even the people.

Soon, the road was more like a river, washing debris up the street as the worm's stance faltered and it looked ready to collapse. Maddie looked to her side, down at the lake of blood, and saw a few more slabs of meat go drifting by, one of which had a small, tired ginger woman sitting on them.

'Fuckin' hell!' they said, with the claw still in their hand. 'That was fun. I kinda wanna go again.'

Maddie rushed over to her, traipsing through all of the blood and worm-skin to grab ahold of her makeshift raft and pull it to the side. She threw her arms around her and hoisted her to her feet.

'Can you stand?' she asked.

Anna flopped to the ground and banged her elbow on the pavement. 'Nope!'

Maddie picked her up again, dragging her to safety as the worm wobbled around, looking for a place to drop dead. It was leaning towards the hospital, and with its size, would have flattened it completely.

'Fall the other way, you fuck!' Anna yelled, resting against Maddie's shoulder. 'Come on, don't be a dick!'

The worm let out one last roar into the clouds before it flopped down in the road and shook the earth; defeated. Its head was right near them, and as Anna drunkenly took out her flashlight, she got a good look at it.

'Jesus Christ, it's hideous,' she said. 'Take me over to it.'

'What?' asked Maddie. 'Why?'

'I wanna get a closer look.'

'You've already been inside of that thing today. Is that not close enough?'

Anna turned to her and looked deep into her eyes. 'Please?'

Maddie sighed. 'Fine,' she said, doing as she was asked.

Up close, Anna hobbled on her own two feet, running her hand gently along the worm's skin as she held her claw tightly with the other. Its eyes up-close were even bigger than she thought – and once the slatted pupil rolled around to look at her – she stared back into one of them for a moment, peacefully.

And then she rammed her claw-spear right into it, twisted it around and yanked it out, bursting the eyeball and covering herself in the juice. The worm was dead.

'Jesus, Anna,' said Maddie.

'EAT SHIT!' she cackled, jabbing the worm's eyeless sockets. 'NOT SO BIG NOW, EH? WOO!'

Maddie gently wrestled the spear away from Anna and took her in her arms. 'Let's take you home now, yeah?' she said.

'I beat it,' Anna replied, trembling. 'I beat the worm. I...'

'I know you did, Anna,' she said, patting her on the head. 'I know.'

'Singlehandedly.'

'I wouldn't go that far.'

'I would.'

'Of course *you* would.'

'Because I'm great.'

'Nope.'

The two giggled with each other.

'Where's Roberto?' Anna asked, arms wrapped around the back of Maddie's neck.

It took Maddie a moment to clock that one. She'd actually gotten a name right.

'I don't know,' Maddie replied, smiling as she turned to look for him. 'I think he went inside. Why'd you ask?'

CHAPTER TWENTY-SIX

DON'T GET INVOLVED

'Whatcha doing?' Anna asked, peering around the corner to Naomi's emergency room where Roberto was sat.

'Bloody hell.' He jolted backwards, almost knocking the heart monitor over. 'You scared me.'

'Mind if I pull up a chair?' she asked.

'Sure.'

Anna looked around. 'There are no chairs in here.'

'Seems that way.'

'Whatever,' she said. 'I'll just sit here.'

She fell face first onto the floor, managed to crawl herself into a ball, and sat cross-legged at Roberto's feet. 'What's up?'

'Nothing,' he said, eyes shifting. 'Just thought I'd sit here for a bit. Everything okay outside?'

'Yeah, think so,' Anna replied. 'Maddie's out there, dealing with all of the human stuff. She didn't trust me with it.'

'She trusted you with me?'

'She doesn't know I'm 'ere.'

'Why are you here?'

Anna looked around. 'I wanted to know why you didn't say anything.'

172 · THOMAS E. STAPLES

Roberto's heart suddenly jittered in his chest. 'Wh-What do you mean?'

'Well, obviously you couldn't tell me. I've been inside a fucking worm for the last couple of hours, but, you could've told Maddie.'

'Told you what?'

She looked right at him, both of their gazes locked. 'Show me your arm.'

'Oh, right,' he sighed. 'That.'

'I'm a detective, Roberto,' she said. 'And I'm not stupid.'

There was a pause.

'Okay, that last part's debatable, but you know what I mean,' she went on. 'When did it happen?'

'I got boxed in by a swarm of little ones,' he said. 'One of them caught me. I just wanted to stay here, with Nay.'

'And wait to die, right?'

'Yeah,' he said. 'And wait to die, just like she will.'

Naomi's body was looking even worse than before. She didn't have long left.

'If you stay,' she said, 'you'll be forced to move outta here when they clear this place out.'

'So?'

'So,' she hauled herself up, grunting along the way. 'Nay dies, and you're still here, waiting for the same.'

'What's the alternative?'

'We lop that bastard arm off and you keep on trucking. Sound good?'

'No.'

'Well, too bad, because we're doin' it anyhow. Come on.'

'Leave me alone.'

'Nope, not happening.'

'Oh for f...' he reached into his pocket, took his wallet out, and handed it over to her. 'Just take it,' he said. 'Take what you need and just leave me alone.'

Anna looked down at the wallet. 'I don't want your money,' she said, slipping it into her pocket. 'I want you to come outta this place, with me, and get that arm looked at.'

'No.'

'Oh, c'mon. Don't be such a...'

'A what? A pussy?'

'No. I wasn't gonna say that. I mean, okay, I might've, but that doesn't mean I was definitely gonna.'

'Please leave, Anna,' he said, looking her in the eye. 'You don't even know me, remember?'

Anna sighed. 'Okay,' she said, staggering to the door and tripping over herself again. 'Fuck sake,' she mumbled. 'Stupid fucking jelly legs sucks fucking dick.'

'Need a hand over there?'

'I got it,' she said, struggling to stand at all. 'You just stay here and, y'know, be sad, and when you're ready to join the rest of us you know where we'll be.'

Roberto went and helped her up, holding her steady. 'There's nothing for me outside of this room,' he said to her.

'Bollocks,' she replied. 'Look, I'm not gonna say that your girl would've wanted you to walk outta this room because I didn't know her, but I don't think anyone would've wanted *this* to happen to you.' She ran her fingers up his bite wound. 'It's not too late,' she said. 'Think about it.'

She took a few steps forward, dragging her face along the wall to keep her balance. Roberto watched her leave, stared at the ground for a moment, and then looked back up to see her still struggling.

Don't get involved, his brain told him. *She'll be fine. They'll be fine.*

'Here,' he said, weaving his arm through hers. 'I'll help you get outside.'

'Oh,' she replied. 'Ta, very much.'

***

The hospital doors slid open to a crowd of people all looking a lot more cheerful than they did a few minutes ago, as Maddie rushed around and made sure everyone was okay, that Bob was okay, and that not a single one of them was going to talk about how good she was with an assault rifle.

That last one was very important.

'It was fucking crazy,' said Bob, chatting to the police sergeant. 'The worm came outta the ground, and then it just kinda fell open and this girl came out with a fucking javelin in her hand or some shit.'

'Uh-huh.'

'You shoulda seen it.'

'I did.'

'Oh. Right, yeah,' he laughed, very awkwardly. 'Hard to miss.'

Bob aborted that conversation quickly and joined the trio as they all tried to stop Anna from slamming headfirst into the concrete steps she was sat on.

'Guys!' Bob called after them. 'Thank you so much for all your help,' he said, eyes darting towards Maddie. 'Especially you.'

He winked. Anna noticed.

'Don't mention it,' Maddie replied.

No, seriously, she thought. *Please don't mention it.*

'I'd be dead if it weren't for you, so, if you ever need anything, please don't hesitate to gimme a call. I'm Bob, by the way.'

'You got a name, Bob?' Anna asked.

'Yeah. I just... What? Is she okay?'

'I think she meant number,' said Maddie. 'She's fine.'

'She's not always like this,' added Roberto. 'Honest.'

'Oh, sure,' he said, scribbling it down on a piece of paper and handing it to her. 'Like I said, anything you need, gimme a bell.'

'Will do,' said Maddie, slipping the number into her pocket. 'Thank you.'

Bob stood himself up straight, saluted the trio, and then left to bug the sergeant some more.

'You ready to go home?' Maddie asked, patting Anna on the shoulder.

'That depends,' she replied, looking over to Roberto. 'Are you heading back?'

He smiled. 'Sure, but first,' he said, rolling up his sleeve. 'I think I'm going to need medical attention.'

'Oh, Christ,' said Maddie, looking shocked. 'How long has—'

'Nope!' Anna barked. 'I've been through this already. You two, bugger off and get that sorted out. I'm gonna chill here for a bit.'

'You sure?' Maddie asked. 'It seems like you've got some new fans.'

Anna nodded. 'Just tell 'em something for me.'

'Oh, god. Here we go. What is it?'

Anna thought about it for a moment. She wanted to ask them all to get their wallets out and hand over their fair share. After all, she saved their lives. She was entitled to a reward of some kind, right?

'Just tell them to take care,' said Anna, 'and that they know where to go if they have any more problems.'

'Really?' Maddie asked. 'No payment?'

'No payment,' she said. 'You remember my email, right? Give 'em that.'

'It's...'

'Anna B. Pendleton, at Gmail dot com.' She clicked her fingers. 'Get on it, buster.'

'Okay, then,' said Maddie, smiling. 'We'll be back soon.'

'I'm sure you will,' she smiled back.

Maddie bent down. 'I love you.'

Roberto audibly gasped.

'I love you, too,' said Anna.

Maddie's eyes looked upwards to Roberto. 'Let's go then.'

The two of them walked away towards the crowd of people.

'Did that just happen?' Roberto whispered. 'Are you two, you know, happening?'

Maddie stopped and looked at him. 'Maybe,' she said. 'Now, let's get that arm seen to.'

CHAPTER TWENTY-SEVEN

CLOSER THAN YOU THINK

'Goddamn, guys,' said Anna. 'These stairs are super uncomfortable. I don't know why I decided to lay here.'

Nobody responded.

'Guys?' she asked. 'Jeez. How long does it take to hand out a few socials and plug my shit?'

She sat upright and looked around her. The car park was empty and all of the lights had been swallowed by a thick, black mist.

'Guys? Are you there?'

The ground all around the steps Anna had been laying on was violently ripped downwards into the darkness, and all that remained was her small and very uncomfortable resting place.

'Oh, shit,' she said, slapping herself in the face. 'Not this again. I wasn't dozing off, I was just resting for a moment. Shit.'

She turned her head, and stood on the steps beside her was a man, covered in black and dripping with shadow.

"Hello, again, Annie,' he said, his voice forever shifting in tone. 'How have you been?'

Anna didn't reply. Those were the rules. Don't reply. Don't talk back. Don't be crazy.

She blinked and the man vanished from sight. Then she felt someone pulling on her hair from behind.

'You've cut it,' the Outsider said. 'I don't like it.'

She spun her head around to face him. There was nobody there. She turned back, and there he was again. His horrible, broken face, with muscle visibly thumping between the cracks in the skin.

'I've been looking for you,' he said. 'Did you notice?'

Anna said nothing.

'Of course, you did,' he sneered. 'You always notice me, Annie.'

He reached out to grab her, and, just like before, she smacked it away; hard. He looked down at his hand with contempt, spat blood onto it, and then smeared it down Anna's face.

She wiped the blood away with her shirt, covering her eyes, and when she could see again, the Outsider had gone.

'I'm still here,' he said, behind her. 'You've been up to a lot recently, haven't you, Annie? Some new friends. Do you like your new friends, Annie? I hope so.'

Anna said nothing.

The ground beneath the Outsider's feet weakened and the concrete crumbled around them.

'Oh dear,' he said. 'I thought we would have longer than this.' He darted towards her, his face inches from hers as he ran his tongue across his jagged teeth. 'I will not stop looking for you. I always find those who owe me something, remember? I will find you, and when I do... Well,' he smirked. 'I really cannot say, now, can I?'

Anna almost said something, but still, said nothing.

'You are not ready for what's coming,' he said, taking a step back. 'Enjoy your friends while you still have them, Annie.'

She looked down. Maddie was lying on the floor, dead, with a deep scar down her cheek. Her stomach had a giant hole in it and her blood leaked down the steps. Roberto, on the other hand, was propped up against the wall with a bullet in his head.

Anna tried to ignore them. They weren't real. None of this was.

'Bad dream, that's all,' said the Outsider, mimicking Anna's voice perfectly, before switching back to a range of them. 'Bad dream. It is time for you to wake up.'

The Outsider turned his back on her and began walking into the distance as smoke billowed from his jacket.

'Giant worm,' Anna whispered. 'Why?'

The Outsider stopped dead at the sound of her voice. 'What?'

'That was you, wasn't it,' she said, not asking. 'All of this. You did this.'

The Outsider was quiet for a moment. 'I didn't. I was just taking advantage of the situation,' he replied. 'Don't you know where the worm came from, Annie?'

Anna suddenly went silent again.

'Oh, dear,' he said, his head jolting to the side to mock her. 'The special girl with the special brain has no clue.'

Don't call me that, she thought, but didn't say.

'Keep out of people's heads,' she sneered. 'I don't know how you're doing it, and I don't care, because I know what you are.'

'Do you, now?'

'Yes,' said Anna.

Slowly cranking his neck around to face Anna, she didn't even flinch when the Outsider dashed right in front of her, tilting his head to the side as he grabbed ahold of hers and dug his fingers into her cheeks. 'Then, what's my name?'

Anna swallowed, hard, and stared into the Outsider's twisted face without an answer.

He released her, but was still leant in close. 'See you soon, Annie.'

Anna was going to let it go. She'd already said too much, but as she leant in, too, she couldn't stop herself. 'Come and get me, then, you fucker,' she said. 'I'll be waiting.'

In an instant, the Outsider and the dream disappeared into the darkness.

***

'Anna?' came Maddie's voice. 'You okay?'

Anna was standing all alone on the steps. She turned around.

'We're going now,' Maddie said. 'They're getting ready to clear the place out. They don't want any of those things wandering around. I told them about that house you visited, and Bob mentioned the sinkhole where he lost his men. Poor guy.'

'So, no more aliens?'

Maddie sighed. 'No more *crabs*, Anna.'

'What about the worm?' she asked. 'It's a bit of a roadblock, innit?'

'I'm sure someone will sort it. Someone who finds their weird little job exciting.' Maddie looked Anna up and down. 'Reminds me of someone.'

'Shut up, you,' said Anna, grinning.

'And, Roberto is very grateful for what you said to him. You brought him around.'

'He's getting it cut off?'

'Seems that way. He said he'll send us pictures, too.'

'Oh, shit. That's gross, dude. I can't wait.'

The two stared at one another in silence for a moment.

'You like me, right?' Anna asked. 'Like, actually. Like, seriously actually?'

'Seriously,' Maddie nodded, holding one of her slime-covered cheeks. 'Seriously actually.'

'But, why? I can't even talk to people. I'm just bad. A big-ass list of bad shit.'

'You'll get there, I promise. There's a good list, too,' said Maddie, 'and I like both of them.'

Anna met her gaze, her face shifting into a grin. 'Okay,' she said. 'Cool. I mean, I wasn't worried or anything. I was just wanted to see if—'

'But I am not kissing that face until you shower. You look like you've been pushed out slowly through a cow's anus, and smell like it, too.'

'That good, huh?'

'Let's go,' said Maddie. 'And check your account when you get home. You may be pleasantly surprised.'

'Wait, really? Who sent...?'

'Check when you get home,' Maddie said, again. 'Come on. Let's get out of here. I'm sick of this place.'

'Where are we going?'

'Well, certainly not back to yours until you get it cleaned up.'

'Oh, okay,' she said. 'So where are we going?'

CHAPTER TWENTY-EIGHT

BITE ME

Madeleine Sandford's apartment wasn't complete and utter shit.

The floor was tidy, there was a giant TV by the back wall, and there was even some actual bloody furniture in the place, too. The carpet, unlike Anna's, had been taken care of, and her living room actually felt like one, being much longer and wider with plenty of space.

'How have I never been here?' Anna asked, careful to not tread worm blood all over the nice carpet.

'You've always been welcome, dummy,' Maddie replied. 'Shower. Now.'

'You're the boss,' said Anna, winking. 'Where is it?'

'Go down the corridor, past the first four doors, and into the one at the end.'

'You have more than one door?' Anna asked. 'What gives? How do you pay for this?'

'Don't worry about it,' she said. 'Coffee?'

'Sure.'

'Nine sugars?'

'Eleven, please.'

Maddie glared at her. 'How many?'

Anna glared back, feeling a little bit intimidated. 'Nine?'

'Better,' she said, flicking the kettle on. 'Meet me in the bedroom when you're done.'

'Ah, we're actually going to make it to a bed this time,' Anna replied, making her voice frighteningly deep. 'You continue to surprise me. Where did innocent Maddie go, eh? I'm used to some big ole wuss flapping off in my earhole every day.'

'I'll show you a big old wuss if you don't get a move on.'

Anna looked around. 'Okay?' she said. 'How does that work? Are you gonna line up a load of people, all proficient in wussiness to a certain degree, and make me guess which wuss is wussier than the other wusses?'

Maddie stared at her, completely unmoving.

'I'm... gonna hop in the shower now,' Anna said.

'Thought so. And check your account.'

'Bite me.'

'Not a bad idea.'

'What?'

'Nothing. Don't worry.'

Anna wandered down the corridor, which was well heated and warmly lit, smelling of lemon and oak, when she fumbled her phone out of her rather sticky pocket and scraped enough of the gunk off to use the screen. She flicked through to her balance and saw a new payment having been made into her account.

Two-hundred and fifty pounds exactly, straight from Roberto's bank.

She reached into her pocket, and Roberto's wallet was gone.

Cheeky bastard, she thought. But she didn't mind, not really, she'd gotten her payment.

Besides, it wasn't all about the money; not anymore.

She passed Maddie's bedroom on the way and had a quick peek inside. It was all perfectly laid out with a made bed, a dim light in the corner and orange LED's around the back wall. A black wardrobe stood high in the corner, pressed up against the dark red walls.

Weirdo, she thought, carrying onwards into the bathroom.

She was going to have time for a better look at the bedroom later, anyway.

***

'You have a nice ceiling,' said Anna, on her back. 'Nicer than mine. How does that happen? How does someone have a nice ceiling?'

Maddie didn't reply. Her mouth was a bit busy at the time, and getting busier.

'Oh, my god,' Anna then groaned, breathing heavy as her head sank into the pillow and she pushed against the headboard. 'Fucking hell.'

A giggle came from under the duvet – from the bump between Anna's legs – before it crawled up her body and Maddie's head popped out.

She wiped her chin. 'All good?'

Anna snorted. 'Don't do that,' she said.

'Do what?'

'Don't make it seem as if my, y'know, stuff was all over your face.'

'It so was.'

'It wasn't!'

'It was, like, everywhere.'

'Stop.'

'All over...'

'You're such an arsehole.'

Maddie slithered up Anna's body and kissed her for a moment, before burying her head against Anna's neck, snuggling up to and wrapping her arms around her.

'How are you feeling?' she asked, gently. 'Thinking you might get some sleep tonight?'

Anna looked up, concerned. 'I'm not sure,' she said. 'Maybe.'

'What are you worried about? It's just a bad dream. Night terrors. You know that.'

'I do,' said Anna, fiddling with Maddie's hair. 'But there's a bit more to it than that and... I dunno. Someone's looking for me and, yeah, I'm worried. It feels real. What if they find me? My address is out there and everything.'

'For now,' said Maddie. 'We'll fix that. Besides, you're safe here, and I think you're going to be getting many more customers now after what happened this week.'

'You think so?'

'Most definitely.'

The two laid together, quietly, as Maddie heard Anna's heart thumping beneath her chest. It was still fast, but, slowing down by the second. It almost sounded normal after a while.

Maddie crawled on top of Anna – just as she was taking in the scent of her coconut shampoo – and looked her in the eye, hands resting on either side of her head. 'You know how you had those spare clothes ready at your place?' she asked. 'The extra toothbrush, extra pillows...'

'Yeah?'

'Was that for me? Were you hoping I'd stay?'

Anna smiled. 'Maybe.'

'That's not a real answer.'

'Well, y'know,' said Anna. 'I had questions, too, remember.'

'Answer mine first, bitch.'

'Fuck off.'

'Never.' Maddie pressed her lips against Anna's, slipping her tongue in, before rolling it down her chin and towards her chest. 'I'm going back down here,' she said. 'Maybe I'll find answers if my aim is good enough.'

And you have no idea how good my aim is, Maddie thought but didn't say.

'Shut up.' Anna laughed. 'You're a twat.'

'Eh. You're the one who'll soon be singing like a canary.'

'Piss off, I will no—oh my god, okay,' she squeaked. 'Stop laughing down there.'

She didn't, not for quite some time.

'You know,' came Maddie's muffled voice. 'You have no real reason to be scared. Not really.'

'Yeah?' said Anna, eyes back on the ceiling. 'Why's that?'

'After all, you took down a giant city-levelling worm in, like, a couple days.'

'Oh yeah,' said Anna. 'And I did it all single-handedly— OW! Don't bite me, you bastard.'

Maddie giggled again. 'But, seriously, think about it.' The duvet came up. 'A giant worm and some crab-monsters,' she said, trying her best to avoid the word alien. 'What can possibly be worse than that?'

EPILOGUE

THE DEATH SQUAD

Andrew only had twenty minutes left on his shift of guard duty, and he wasn't going to survive many more of them.

The snow made it tough for Andrew to see anything beyond a few feet in front of him, and made holding his rifle still even harder. His gloves were thick and heavy, as was the rest of his jet black combat uniform. The mask he had was almost entirely reflective, so he could've been mistaken for any of the other fifty-plus guards that worked at the Black Mask facility.

The place needed all of the defences it could muster.

Andrew walked back and forth just ahead of the gate that led into the main area of the compound. Another guard was there, just as faceless and unrecognisable as all the others, which was perhaps the point, but Andrew still knew their name.

'You wanted to take that break, still?' said Andrew. He had a Canadian accent, which wasn't surprising considering he was just outside of Quebec.

'Sure,' Katie replied, the other guard. 'I really need the bathroom.'

'Go on, then,' said Andrew, nodding his head off to the side. 'Go through the back way, and don't take too long.'

She nodded in return. 'I won't,' she said, walking out of sight.

Andrew looked forward, straight up the road ahead, and saw a figure slowly drift its way through the blizzard. It could've been anyone at that distance, and they weren't showing any signs of aggression, so Andrew took it easy.

'Hey there!' he called out, shouting over the heavy winds. 'What's your business here?'

The figure got nearer, still not in full clarity until they were a couple of meters away from Andrew. Once they were, he saw them dressed from head to toe in a long grey cloak, with a bright light burning outwards from where their eyes would've been.

It was bright red; a horizontal strip of light embedded into a metallic, pristine faceplate.

'You don't wanna be out here,' said Andrew, fumbling with his rifle. 'It's cold. Cool mask, by the way.'

The figure kept walking, so Andrew raised his gun.

'Okay, you can stop there,' he said. 'You obviously don't work here, so I'll need you to turn around and head back the way you came. Do it now, please.'

They didn't, but they had, at last, stopped moving.

'Sir, or Madame, if you do not turn around and leave, I will be forced to open fire.'

Still nothing.

'I can promise that if I have to shoot you,' said Andrew. 'I will not miss.'

He felt something warm in his chest, then. A sudden jolt that'd spread across his entire body, and when he looked down at his stomach, he noticed it had a four-foot long blade sticking right through it.

He dropped his gun as the sword was wrenched out of his chest and he fell to his knees, spitting blood into his mask. He looked behind him, seeing someone wearing almost identical gear to the red-faced figure, but not standing anywhere near as tall and with a green light on their mask, instead.

They cocked their head to the side and watched as Andrew tried to crawl away, unable to scream loud enough for anybody to hear him over the blizzard. He dragged himself around the side entrance, leaving a trail of blood behind him, hoping to find Katie as he went.

He did, and she was dead, too.

A third person stood next to her corpse, which had been strung up on the wall with Katie's own large intestine wrapped around her neck; the small one still hanging out of her hollow belly, dripping blood onto the snow.

The killer turned to Andrew, looking at him with their own mask. It was pristine and silver, just like the others, with a blue strip of light running across it to form the eye of a cyclops. They walked towards Andrew, and then just stepped right over him.

He was Green's kill, after all.

Andrew rolled over, vomiting blood onto the inside of his visor until Green crouched over him and took it from his face. He held up his index finger and pressed it to Andrew's lips, before taking it away and waggling it left and right.

'Who are you?' Andrew asked, choking.

Green didn't answer, before swiping his blade across Andrew's throat and tearing it wide open, spraying blood onto his uniform and the ground below.

He lied there for a moment, bleeding to death as the encompassing white abyss of the snow only got whiter, all while the three light-faced killers stormed into the compound. He sat up against the wall, fading, when he saw a word painted onto the one opposite in blood.

Who's blood? He wasn't sure, Katie's probably. It wasn't a word he recognised, either. But, as he drifted off into the dark, that word was the last thing he ever saw.

Pendleton.

THE BEGINNING

I love monsters. Fictional ones, of course, and if you've made it this far, reader, then I'd like to think that you love them, too. I've wanted to write about them since I was six years old, and now, in your hands, fourteen years later, is the result.

I won't keep you for long, as this novel that you've just read through is all about keeping the pace going, and I want to continue that here.

My aim was to evoke the feeling of a story that's been thrown against your face really hard as you go about your day, and after taking a moment to compose yourself and having hopefully enjoyed the experience in some way, you'll ask a bunch of questions like:

"What's happening next?"

"Is there more to come?"

And...

"Why is this random guy throwing shit at me?"

Well, before I answer your questions in the oddly specific order you asked them in, reader, I would like to first ask for your help.

This book is self-published. I paid for the editor – the excellent Kathleen Howard, who did a magnificent job of pointing me in the right direction – and the cover artist – the wonderful Ivan Cakic Cakamura, who absolutely nailed my creative vision and is just generally really talented and lovely – whereas the rest was done by me. If you enjoyed this book, and I sincerely hope you did, it would mean the world to me if you could leave a review on Amazon, Goodreads, or your local toilet cubicle wall.

Don't actually do that last one. Vandalism is really bad, guys.

By purchasing this book you have already done something that means so much to me, which is more than enough on your end. But, anything that you can do to help spread the word about this book would be incredibly helpful, as well. If you simply recommend it to somebody that you think would enjoy it and they end up snagging a copy or even borrowing yours, you are then responsible for having doubled the number of people who have read this book in comparison to how many wrote it.

That's crazy.

Next, you can follow me on my Twitter: @MrTEStaples.

I don't tweet much, but I'm often active on there. It's one of the best ways to reach me and, again, if you liked what you read, I would love to hear from you.

I'm particularly susceptible to photos of my book – or device containing said book – taken with the various pets that you may have, and if you're unable to do that... I dunno. Take a photo of it looking all cosy on the sofa with a cup of tea or something? That'd be cute.

So, what's happening next? Well...

As you have most likely already guessed by the giant "1" on the spine of this book, or by the way it says the word "One" on the title page, this is the first in a series.

It is *A Pendleton Case*, after all, of which there will be more.

In the future – the near future, I might add – you can expect more over-the-top horror, jokes and, of course, monsters; all with the companionship of the new couple to keep you company.

Because, yes, Anna Pendleton and Madeleine Sandford will return.

I hope that you'll stick around for that, as this is just the beginning, and I can't wait to take you on this crazy, terrifying, and exciting adventure with me.

So, I guess I can't answer that last question for you, but I don't think I'll need to. All I can do is promise that I won't throw the next one at you quite as hard, but, just as a precaution, be ready to catch it in case I do.

I'll let you go now, although I hope to see you again someday.

Take care, reader. Until next time...

Thomas E. Staples
24th of January, 2019

ABOUT THE AUTHOR

Thomas E. Staples is a University student currently studying Creative Writing. With a love of both horror and comedy, they often smash the genres together very irresponsibly to see what happens. They have published multiple short stories since 2015, started writing books, too, apparently, and find talking about themselves in the third-person incredibly awkward.

The Case of the Giant Carnivorous Worm is their debut novel.

They can be reached on Twitter - @MrTEStaples - or via their website www.wrybrain.com.

Made in the USA
Middletown, DE
25 May 2021